KYLAN

THE WYLDE STREET BOYS SERIES
BOOK 3

N.R. WALKER

COPYRIGHT

Cover Artist: Pretty in Ink Designs
Editor: Boho Editing
Publisher: BlueHeart Press
Kylan © 2025 N.R. Walker
The Wylde Street Boys Series © 2025 N.R. Walker

WARNING

Intended for an 18+ audience only. This book contains material that is intended for a mature, adult audience. It contains graphic adult situations.

TRADEMARKS

All trademarks are the property of their respective owners.

BLURB

Kylan Grant finds solace and comfort in the arms of strange men. He learned early on—far earlier than most—that the fleeting attention and adoration of older men made him feel wanted. Attention he never got anywhere else. Attention he craves. Attention he gets from his two daddies.

Leon Ellington and Marek Akhurst met in college and have been inseparable since. Now in their late forties and married, they're the formidable names behind some of the most lucrative and savage legal cases in the country.

They live together, work together, and play together. What one wants, the other acquires; whatever the urge, whatever the whim. Whatever the cost.

What they want is Kylan.

And what Kylan gets out of it is worth more than the money they pay him.

But as the lines between fantasy and reality begin to blur, they soon realise there was nothing in their contract about falling in love.

CAUTION WARNING

kylan

book three

N.R. WALKER

ONE
KYLAN GRANT

I WELCOMED the calm that washed through me the second I walked through the front door. Leon and Marek's house was a mansion in one of Sydney's most expensive suburbs. Ridiculous in its opulence, it had Leon's touch in the vast open spaces, marble floors and black fixtures, and Marek's design touch on all the extravagant furnishings. Velvet settees with gilded carved wood, dark walls and rich leathers, fur and feathers and fine touches.

Magnificent, luxurious.

Expensive.

Amounts of money that I couldn't fathom.

Most people probably felt overwhelmed in their house.

I felt nothing but peace.

"Are you okay, darling?" Marek asked.

I gave a nod and smiled for him. "Yes. Much better now I'm here."

He gently touched my cheek. "Sweet boy. Run along upstairs. Come down when you're ready. Leon will be down shortly."

I gave a nod and went up to my room.

My room, it was called, though it wasn't really my room at all. It was one of the spare bedrooms where I changed clothes, showered if needed, and slept in on the odd occasion.

I could leave my bag in there, which was nice. But it wasn't really *my* room.

Nothing in this house was mine.

Not even the two men who lived here.

Especially not the two men who lived here.

They belonged only to each other. I was a whim, they'd said, way back when this agreement began. A tasty treat to be shared between husbands.

I didn't care what they called me. Not back then. For the amount of money they paid me—for what they did to me, did to my body, and what they did for my mind—they could call me whatever they wanted.

It wasn't a hardship. It wasn't something I had to endure. It was the opposite of that.

They gave me peace.

They quietened the noise in my head. They stripped away all the bullshit of my life and gave me peace.

The mental headspace I craved, that I needed.

The fact they paid me for it was a bonus.

I'd do it for free.

Hell, I'd pay them if I had the money.

Like a junkie paying for a fix, that's how much I needed this.

The wardrobe drawers were empty save the top one. It was mine also, containing the few things they kept here for me.

The clothes they liked me to wear.

That *I* liked to wear.

That I felt adored in.

I felt pretty.

The way they fussed over me, caressed me, whispered sweet things, called me nice names.

I loved all of it.

Especially the way they fucked me while I wore them.

I loved that the most.

I was their femboy. Their pretty boy. Their princess.

Lacey underwear, sometimes a negligee, sometimes a garter belt with stockings. Sometimes it was just a very short cotton skirt, the girly kind that lifted when I twirled. The kind they could easily lift when they fucked me. Sometimes I wore glittery eyeshadow and lip gloss, but not all the time.

Sometimes I painted my nails for them. Sometimes they painted them for me.

I loved how they pampered me, adored and cherished me.

Wanted me.

I chose the plain blue cotton skirt for today. It was short enough to see my lacey arseless underwear if I perked my arse up enough, and I added a touch of pink lip gloss to my lips. But my favourite part was the vibrating butt plug.

I was tempted to turn it on, but no . . . that was not for me to decide. Not today. I wanted my daddy to decide for me.

I took the remote control and went downstairs. The butt plug felt amazing, the anticipation building . . . I was so ready. I was almost buzzing with knowing what was in store.

I was desperate for it. I needed them to have me. All weekend if they wanted, as many times as they were able.

"Oh, here he is," Leon said. "Come over here, boy." He was sitting on the double seater in the living room. Marek sat in the single chair next to him.

I flittered over, quick, small steps so my skirt swished, and I went to kneel on the floor between them, which was usually how these things started.

But Leon patted the seat next to him. "Sit here, darling."

Fear struck me. Panic and unease clawed at my throat.

Marek softened. "Oh, you're not in any trouble, sweet boy," he said, standing up to take my hand and help me sit next to Leon. "We just want to talk."

"Did I . . . did I do something wrong?" I asked, my hands wringing knots in my lap. I felt ill, dread roiling a greasy swell in my belly.

"Not at all," Leon said.

He was the stricter of the two. Stern, straight-backed,

and serious. Whereas Marek was softer and comforting, Leon was self-composed and a touch austere.

He wasn't cruel or uncaring. Not at all. He was just rigid. When he gave praise, I relished in it.

"You know Dominic Lowing and Nolan O'Brien," Leon said.

My eyes went to his. *Dominic and Nolan* . . . "Yes."

"They mentioned you to us last night," Marek added gently. "Showed us a photo, actually. To see our reaction."

"A photo?" I asked. "I didn't . . ."

Leon raised his hand. "It's fine. Dominic was very quick to assure us you gave nothing away, and you refused to confirm or deny."

"I would never," I said, looking between them. "I would never jeopardise this. What you two do for me is . . . I would never breach the NDA. I haven't even told Benji or Fitch anything." I shook my head. "When Nolan mentioned your names to Dominic, I was stunned. I didn't mean to give anything away. I just wasn't prepared. I will try harder next time. I should have expected it, though. I knew they went to Club 180 and . . . I should have expected and been better prepared—"

Leon slid his hand over mine. "It's okay, darling," he murmured. "You're not in trouble. You didn't breach anything. We just wanted to let you know that we know to and ask if you had any questions or concerns."

I shook my head. "No. None. Who you know is not my concern. I don't care if you know them or even if you like them or not. It doesn't change anything for me."

Marek smiled. "We like them just fine."

"You've been to Nolan's place?" Leon pushed. "That's where the photo was taken."

I nodded. "Many times. It's where Benji's staying, so we go there to see him. But Nolan's not even there most of the time. We just go and hang out. On the balcony, usually. I've never been to Dominic's house. I have no reason to go there."

"It's okay," Marek said. He came to kneel in front of me. "You're not in any trouble. We just wanted to hear it from you, and now we all know about it, there'll be no more surprises, okay?" He fixed my skirt and gave me a smile. "Nothing changes here, okay? You felt anxious and thought you were in trouble?"

I nodded, feeling better but still a little uneasy. "Yes."

"You didn't like it, did you?" Leon asked.

I shook my head quickly. "No. I thought you were going to terminate the contract. I don't want to displease you. Either of you," I said, looking at Marek. "I need this. What you both do for me."

Marek smiled up at me. "I know you do. You need it like we need it."

Leon hummed. "Do you feel better now, sweet boy?"

I nodded quickly and gave him a smile. "Yes, thank you."

He looked at my hands. "What have you got there?"

I opened my hand to show him the small remote control on my palm. Leon took it. "Ah, I see. Would you like me to activate it for you, sweetheart?"

My breath left me in a rush of relief. "Yes, please. Should I kneel on the floor for you, daddy?"

Marek put his hands on my knees and spread them. His eyes went to my lace-covered cock. "No need, pretty boy. Not this time."

Leon lifted the remote control and switched it on.

TWO
MAREK AKHURST

NOTHING TURNED me on more than watching Leon work Kylan over.

When he activated the vibrating butt plug, the way Kylan arched and threw his head back. The way he welcomed the sensation, how his entire body reacted. His skin prickled all over, his nipples pebbled, his neck corded, his mouth open, eyes closed, hands clawing at the sofa.

And the way Leon teased him, lightly skimming his hands over Kylan's chest, his tiny waist, making Kylan hiss and whimper.

When he tweaked his nipples, kissed him deeply, rubbed the lace that barely contained him, rattled the butt plug before pulling it out. The way that boy arched his back, yearning for more, begging and pleading for Leon to please, please fuck him.

And my god, the way Leon lifted that pretty skirt and sunk his cock into that tight little arse.

The way Kylan gasped and moaned, almost sobbing with sweet relief as Leon began to fuck him. Slow at first, but long and deep, taking him to that place he needed to be.

That place where nothing existed but pleasure and praise. It was a high, an ecstasy he could get nowhere else.

I understood that all too well. So did Leon.

It was why we chose Kylan.

The first time had been a one-off fluke. We'd been at 180 and walked out to find a petite boy on the corner of Wylde and Oxford. We'd asked him if he'd be interested in double the money and he was more than eager.

And earn his money, he did.

What we'd found was a boy who fit our list of needs so well, we eventually made it a weekly fix. In fact, he was so fucking perfect for us we made it a twice a week contract.

We liked a pretty little thing that we could share, that would welcome both of us, that we could dress up and pamper, then do all kinds of heavenly things to.

The thing about Kylan was, we soon learned, that he needed it as much as we did.

It was so easy to see how pretty he felt, how happy he was. Putting on a tiny skirt that twirled or pretty knickers and stockings.

Just like it was easy to see how much pleasure he got out of it. Having one of our cocks buried inside him while the other watched, or when we spit-roasted him—which was clearly his favourite—sent Kylan to his happy place.

He got that glazed-over look on his face, in his eyes; satisfaction, relief, pride.

He was born to be a femboy.

Our femboy.

He thrived.

And watching Leon fuck him gave me a great sense of pleasure and pride as well. We'd always included a third in our bed for the pure satisfaction of watching the man we loved most in this world in his element.

Leon was a god amongst men.

To me, at least.

I adored him, loved him more than life itself, and watching him fuck another man turned me on in ways I couldn't explain.

Almost more than when he fucked me.

And I know he got off on watching me fuck Kylan as well.

He was never sexier than with a femboy between us.

I fucking loved it.

This beautiful boy. So pretty, so fem, so eager to please.

His entire purpose was to please us, and in return we spoiled him, pampered him, cherished him.

Gave him pleasures he never knew possible.

But more than that, we took his mind to places he needed to go.

I could see it in his eyes when he reached that place of bliss. When Leon pumped his seed into him, Kylan gasped, smiling, over-awed, and his eyes . . . glazed over with pride and pleasure.

When it was my turn, Leon sat on the bed, leaning against the headboard, Kylan's face buried in his chest, body between his thighs while I got into position.

Leon kissed him softly, stroking his cheek. "Good boy," he murmured. "You like to please your daddies, don't you, boy?"

Kylan nodded.

I held Kylan's hips and inspected his hole. He was gaping open, Leon's come trickling at the edge, and absolutely glorious. "Ready for your second daddy?" I asked.

Kylan nodded again and Leon held him to his chest while I raised his hips. "That's it, boy," Leon cooed. "Keep your little arse up for him. Let him in."

Sliding into Kylan was heaven and ecstasy all in one. Even with Leon opening him up, he was still tight. Warm, wet, and full of my lover's seed. Knowing I was fucking Leon's come into him was a level of devotion I couldn't find anywhere else.

The way we shared this boy, the way we adored him equally. His small arse, his narrow hips fit in my hands so perfectly. I could grip him and fill him so thoroughly. He lay on Leon's chest, cradled in his strong arms, his face in Leon's chest hair as he took every inch of me.

Kylan whined and moaned, and I pressed my weight down on him. Leon's arms slid around me, his eyes locked with mine over Kylan's head, and he held us both as I began the slow climb to climax.

We sandwiched him, held him between us, as I thrust long and deep. Just how he loved it. His moans became louder, sharper, and he tried to roll his hips, tried to move.

Leon held him tighter.

"Does this feel good, boy?" Leon asked.

"Yes," he cried.

"You like it when your daddies do this to you, don't you, boy?"

He whined, an almost-sob. "Yes."

Leon's eyes never left mine. "I think our boy is about to come," he murmured. "His cock is hard, rubbing against mine."

"I'm gonna come soon," I whispered. "He feels so good. Love fucking your come into him. Turns me on so much."

Leon's sultry smirk curled my insides, warm and lovely. "God, I fucking love you," he murmured. "Love watching you fuck him. Love it when he's between us like this."

Kylan cried out, his small body stiffening and shuddering between us as he came. His arse clenched around my cock, milking me, and it brought me undone. Too much pleasure, too many sensations, so much love in Leon's eyes as he watched me come.

I thrust into Kylan hard, holding his hips firm, and pumped my load deep inside him. I collapsed on top of him, his body wracked with aftershocks and soft whimpers, ragged breathing, and Leon's hands on my sides, in my hair.

I never felt closer to Leon than I did in that moment. In every moment like this. When we shared Kylan, when we watched each other. The eye contact, the indulgence, the hedonism.

And sweet, sweet Kylan . . .

He was limp and pliable, sated and adored.

I pulled out of him and ran my hands over his back before kissing his shoulder. "Are you okay there, sweet boy?"

He chuckled out a sigh. "Yes, daddy. Never better, daddy."

Leon stroked Kylan's hair. "You made a mess on me, boy."

"Sorry, daddy," he replied. "I couldn't help it. It feels so good when you press me between you. When you both want me at the same time."

I sat back on my haunches and spread his arse cheeks. He was well used, and the mix of our come was leaking out.

"So beautiful." My spent cock twitched. "Fuck, I almost wanna go again."

"I'll take more, daddy," Kylan said. "Whenever you want me."

Twenty years ago, I would have. I'd have fucked him three or four times in one night. But as willing as I was, forty-seven-year-old me wasn't as capable.

Leon chuckled and lifted Kylan's chin, bringing him in for a kiss. "Greedy boy."

Kylan nodded. "I want to make you happy," he said earnestly.

"You do, darling," I murmured. "But we should shower, clean us all up."

I knew Leon wouldn't love having that come dry on his skin. Not that he was a neat freak or a germaphobe. He just preferred to be tidy, organised, and clean.

I helped Kylan kneel on the bed, and I held his hand as he climbed off and got to his feet. I lifted his chin and kissed him softly. "You're such a good boy."

He preened. "Thank you, daddy."

Then I held out my hand for Leon, and as he sat on the edge of the bed, I brought his hand to my lips and kissed his knuckles. "My king."

He laughed as he stood up, kissing me soundly. "My king," he said back to me. Then he kissed Kylan. "And our pretty princess."

He revelled in our praise.

Our shower was a large walk-in with double detachable showerheads. Lavish and pretentious, maybe, but then again, this whole house was.

So were we.

We were indulgent. We liked the finer things.

Like Kylan.

We showered him, bestowing him with gentle caresses and soft kisses. My god, how he shined.

Compared to when we first met him, first had him. That Kylan had been rigid and scared, unsure of what we might do, or if we might hurt him. He'd been in a permanent state of fight or flight, it seemed. Like a bird brought in from a storm.

Now he was free. Free to be himself, free to be touched and kissed, free to feel safe and cherished.

He radiated contentment the second he walked through our door. The change in him was day and night.

He felt safe here and secure.

No one could hurt him. Or worse . . .

Two nights per week, he was with us, and we wished it was more. But we travelled with work, and we had late nights, early mornings. And some nights we needed to unwind with a few drinks at 180, just the two of us.

But these nights with Kylan had brought us closer, and I wasn't sure how that was even possible. Leon and I were watertight. Always had been. Never one moment of doubt, never one argument. Since we met all those years ago.

Yet somehow this boy had brought a new element to us, to our relationship, to our home, and to our bed.

A nurturing side, where we could watch each other thrive and grow with kindness and adoration—and smoking hot sex—with another man. Where Kylan was the conduit for mine and Leon's love for one another.

A much younger man. A twink with a slight build and a big heart. A femboy who needed so much love and attention it took two daddies.

"Here he is," Leon said. We were standing in our kitchen, wearing our lounge pants and not much else, waiting for Kylan to come downstairs. He was wearing my silk robe, undone of course, small black panties, and soft black dainty slippers.

His hair was still damp, neatly brushed to one side, and a touch of pink lip gloss. He was shower-fresh, his clean skin flushed pink.

"You look beautiful," I whispered, running my thumb along his jaw. "Beautiful enough to eat."

Leon chuckled. "We need to feed him first. I thought I'd make you a nice salad with sliced steak. How does that sound?" he asked Kylan.

Leon loved to cook and potter around the kitchen. He spoiled us both.

"It sounds amazing," Kylan replied softly, sliding his arms around him and giving Leon a cuddle. "Thank you, daddy."

"Hm," he said, flustered by the attention, but the hint of his smile gave him away. "Now be a good boy and do some reading while I make us dinner."

"Need me to help with anything?" I asked him.

Leon leaned over and kissed me. "No, love. Go and sit with him in case he has any questions."

I took Kylan's hand and led him to the study. He knew the routine. He knew where his books were and where he was up to.

Was this part of our agreement?

No, not in our contract anyway.

But he'd shown interest and ability, so it was a natural progression. We made it a point of doing this once a week, and Kylan was advancing well.

Kylan went to his seat and opened his first book. He looked so quaint in the robe and slicked down hair, his rosy cheeks and shiny lips. Like a star from the silver screen.

Just gorgeous.

I kissed the side of his head. "I wish you could see

how beautiful you are right now," I whispered. He made my heart swell with affection, and pleasure pooled in my belly. Leon and I had often spoken of the constant attraction toward him, the constant sexual desire, the need to act out every impulse, every whim.

"I'd ask you to sit on my lap," I murmured, unable to take my eyes off him. "But I fear you won't get much homework done."

He looked up from his book, mischief tugging at his smile, then stood up with his book in hand and walked over to me. His robe fell open all the way, his panties barely concealed anything; his long, lean thighs and small waist took my breath away.

Then he sat on my lap, making no attempt to conceal himself with his robe, and opened his book.

"Can you help me read, daddy?" he asked shyly while pressing against my crotch.

Little minx.

"Of course, princess," I said. I took a look at the chapter heading he was starting from and read it out loud. "Statutory interpretation: Principles and Context, Chapter Eight."

THREE
KYLAN

WHEN I'D FIRST AGREED to the contract terms and conditions with Leon and Marek, I assumed it would be for sex and role playing only.

And for the first few sessions, it was.

And it was fucking amazing.

But with the introduction of the NDA and legal jargon, I'd asked questions. And, apparently, I'd asked the right questions because Leon and Marek were impressed. One thing led to another, and before I knew it, they were incorporating quiet reading time into my time with them.

It didn't cut into our sex and role playing. It just got factored in. We'd usually have round one as soon as I arrived, then take a break to shower, eat, and sit around their study or lounge room with a book before round two began.

They were both property lawyers and incredibly smart, so they loved being able to sit on their chesterfield sofas, reading legal and finance journals like real daddies while their princess lay on the floor in his robe, on his tummy with his legs kicking.

It was fun at first, all part of the role playing. Until I started actually reading and understanding their textbooks. They encouraged me to read their old law textbooks, and I'd annotate and diarise, make notes and write essays.

I wouldn't say I enjoyed the reading part of my time with them *more* than the sex, because that'd be a lie. But I really did enjoy it. I looked forward to it, even.

The fact they were impressed with my work made me so freaking happy. The rush of pride and fulfilment was almost the same high as when they praised me for being a good boy while they took turns fucking me.

Almost.

That high would never be beaten.

My god, I loved it.

I loved wearing silk and satin. I loved how it felt on my skin. I loved wearing small heeled slippers with an open robe. I felt like a Playboy bunny. Sexy, desirable, wanted.

Plus, it drove Leon and Marek crazy, to the point of distraction. To the point of insanity. Until they couldn't stand it anymore and would bend me over the nearest piece of furniture. Or on the floor, or on the stairs, or in their car.

Wherever the need arose.

I couldn't get enough of them either.

It was a mutual need.

And I appreciated them each equally. I didn't favour

one over the other. They were both on par, both different in their own ways, and I needed them both.

I could watch Benji with Nolan for the sweetness and Fitch with Dominic for the sensual heat, but with Leon and Marek, I got both.

I wished I could tell Benji and Fitch about them. About what we did, the glorious fucking and the reading.

But I would never jeopardise the NDA. I would never give them reason to end it.

Which is why I almost died when they brought up the NDA and me knowing Nolan and Dominic. Panic had ripped through me, squeezing my heart to the point of physical pain.

I might have realised something then.

Something I'd witnessed recently with both Benji and Fitch . . . how they felt about Nolan and Dominic. How they'd both been so panicked at the idea of ending things with them, because they were in love.

It felt far too familiar.

Did I love Leon and Marek?

I loved what they did to me, what they did for me. But I wasn't sure I was capable of love.

Or worthy.

And I highly doubted they'd reciprocate it.

They were in love with each other. They told each other often and it made my heart pang with jealousy and want.

I had no doubt that they loved their time with me, they loved fucking me, they loved the feminine-boy body

I gave them. I was their toy thing, their object to adore and use as they saw fit.

They loved all those things.

But could they ever love me?

Could anyone?

Fitch knocked on my door, startling me, and poked his head in. "Hey."

I was glad for the distraction before I could spiral any further. "Hey, wassup?"

"I finished filming my first solo," he said, cringing. "Jesus. Will this get easier? Please tell me it'll get easier."

I smiled at him. "I'm sure it will."

One corner of his mouth pulled down with uncertainty. "So, do I edit it? I did a quick check to make sure my face is kept out of it."

We had the lighting and the angles all worked out. We knew where we could lie, kneel, and sit on the bed while keeping our faces out of it.

"I can take a look if you want," I said.

I had no qualms in seeing them do their thing. We were all sex workers, and I'd seen them both work before. I'd seen their junk. Hell, I'd seen it all.

I had no issue with them watching my videos either.

I was used to being watched while I got railed. Both Leon and Marek took any inhibitions I had and whittled them down to nothing.

Fitch laughed. "If you wanna jerk off to my videos, you can pay to subscribe."

I snorted. "Fuck off."

His smile faded away with a sigh. "Well, I guess if

we're gonna do this and make a fuckton of money, we need to get used to seeing each other's videos, right?"

I shrugged. "It will help keep us familiar too, so we know not to double up and get repetitive. We should keep a list."

"A list of what?"

"What we do, what clothes we wear, what toys we use, how long each video is." I shrugged again. "That way we can see which are our most popular videos and see at a glance why it worked and maybe why some don't."

He studied me for a second. "You're good at this. You know that, right?"

I grinned at him. "I'm good at a lot of things."

"I bet you are," he murmured, nudging me with his elbow. "Taking two daddies at once. You know, that's something I've never done."

"What? Had a threesome?"

"Well, threesome, sure. But never a DP."

I frowned at him, unsure of just how much I could divulge. Surely saying what I had and hadn't done during sex without mentioning any names or details wasn't in breach of anything . . .

"Neither have I," I said.

His gaze shot to mine, excitement lighting up his whole face. "Oh my god, is that an *actual* detail?" Then he stopped. "Wait. What do you mean you've never had a DP? You have two daddies. Do you mean to tell me you've been their boy toy for months and you've never had both their dicks in you at the same time?"

I didn't need to answer that because I technically already had.

Fitch deflated. "I don't know if I'm sad or disappointed."

I snorted. "The fact you feel anything about my sex life is both sad and disappointing."

He shoved me. "Oh, shut up. You never give details. Ever. So this little snippet of news is a big deal for me."

I sighed and pressed Play on Fitch's video.

The opening shot was of the bed and Fitch stepping into view. He wore small underwear . . . no, not just underwear, but dinosaur underwear and a crop top that barely covered his nipples.

"Dinosaurs? Really?"

He nodded as if it were the most normal thing in the world. "Stegosauruses. Dom bought them for me."

I smiled at that.

"I don't know if I would enjoy a DP," he volunteered. "I'd only want it if it was Dominic anyway, so unless he has a clone, it's a moot point. Not that I could fit two of Dominic's dicks in me anyway. One is big enough. And it's never gonna happen with someone else, so . . ."

I watched on-screen as he knelt on the bed, side view to the camera, and rested on his haunches. No face visible, no details. The angle looked good. He then took his prostate wand and slicked it up with lube.

"Daddy likes it when I'm ready for him," on-screen Fitch said.

"So when you're with your two daddies," beside-me Fitch said. "They don't fuck you at the same time?"

"You could get a silicone mould of his dick," I suggested. "Then you'd technically have two of his dicks to fuck you."

He raised an eyebrow at me. "That's a good idea. Still not sold on the DP, but if I could keep it here and use it on the nights I don't see him . . ." He grinned. "That's a great idea, Ky. I'm gonna ask him."

I snorted. Because of course he would.

On-screen Fitch raised up on his knees a little, moved his underwear to one side and slipped the lubed-up wand into his arse. "Oh, daddy," he murmured on-screen.

"Is that too much?" he asked beside me.

' People are gonna love this," I admitted.

We watched as he rocked up and down a little, working the wand all the way in. The skin on his thighs had goosebumps, his hands caressed his tummy, his nipples.

"They take turns," I admitted, answering his earlier question. I made sure not to look at him, keeping my eyes on the screen. "They don't fuck me at the same time. Maybe one will hold me, wrap me up in their arms so I can't move while the other one fucks me. Then they take turns."

I could feel Fitch staring at me. "Fuck, that's hot."

Hell yes, it was.

"Or they'll spit-roast me," I added.

"Oh fuck, yes," Fitch whispered. "Tell me everything."

I smiled. "I can't."

He sighed quietly and we watched the screen. On-screen Fitch picked up the small remote pad and pressed it on. A quiet buzz was drowned out by his yelp as he rose to his knees. We could see the wand protruding from his arse that way, as his hips jerked forward. His erection barely contained in those small, boy underwear.

"Okay, so Dom helped me practice with the wand," he said. "But damn. What have I been missing all this time? Needless to say, he ordered one to keep at his place."

I chuckled, but this surprised me. I looked at him then. "You've never used them before?"

"Never," he said. "You have?"

"All the time." I shrugged. "Mostly vibrating butt plugs. And one of them keeps the controls."

He threw his head back and groaned. "Fuck yes. Now we're talking."

I shook my head, having already said too much. "You cannot repeat anything I tell you."

He mimicked locking his lips and throwing away the key. "But I'm storing it away in my spank bank."

I shoved him again. "You're such a whore."

"I know," he said. "I fucking love it."

We went back to watching on-screen Fitch. His thighs were trembling now, his hips jerking forward, the head of his cock peeking out of his briefs with every thrust, slick with precome.

"Oh daddy, please stop," on-screen Fitch cried out. "It's too much. I can't take it, please stop."

But then his hands gripped his thighs, fingers clawing

at the skin, and he screamed as he came. Come shot from his cock, the camera catching every spurt.

His hands shook, his thighs trembled, and his arse quivered as he turned the wand off. He gasped and moaned, and then, like the absolute little whore he was, he ran his hand through his come, painting it on his abs, and through his ragged breaths, he spoke in a soft, boy voice. "Oh, daddy, I made a mess."

I snorted out a laugh and nudged him with my elbow. "You're a filthy little fucker."

He laughed without shame. "Dom loves it when I say that. I swear to god, he goes crazy. You should totally use that line when your daddies make you come; see how they react. You can thank me later."

I shook my head at him, pretending that I'd do no such thing, but in reality, I just might . . .

On-screen Fitch stood up off the bed and turned the camera off. "So whaddya think? Good, bad. Can we use it?"

I turned to look at him then. "That was perfect. They're gonna love you. If you can do something like that every time, you'll be raking in the money."

He grinned at me. "Can I show it to Dom? Like a preview, test-viewing type thing?"

"For his pleasure? Or his approval?" I didn't know why I said that, and I regretted it the second it was out of my mouth.

"Both," he replied quietly. "I want his approval. In everything." He studied me for a second. "Are you telling me you don't strive for your daddies' approval? You want to make them proud of you, right?"

I let out a sigh and answered with a nod. "Sorry. I didn't mean for it to sound like it did. Of course I want them to approve . . ." I sighed again, more in frustration this time.

I'd always loved the fact I was gagged by the NDA. I could keep all the details to myself, a gift just for me, not to be shared with anyone else.

I shared my body with strangers for money. I shared enough.

My time with Leon and Marek had always been just mine.

But now I'd divulged a few small nondescript things to Fitch . . . I wanted to tell him more.

I wanted to tell Fitch how happy I was. How happy they made me. I wanted to tell him about my studies, how they encouraged me to be better, to want better *of* myself and *for* myself.

I wanted to tell him how much I loved them both, and how it killed me that they were so in love without me. How they were the best thing to happen to me in years, how they encouraged me to dress up and feel pretty. How I wanted them to keep me forever.

But I couldn't.

I couldn't say any of that.

"Yeah," I whispered. "Show Dom. Let me know what he thinks, but I'm pretty sure we both know he's gonna love it."

Fitch winced. "Hey, I'm sorry. I shouldn't have asked questions. I didn't mean to ruin your mood."

I tried to smile for him. "Nah, it's all good. I can't talk about them. I shouldn't have said anything . . ." I clapped his shoulder. "Your video was great. The lighting was good, the angle and side view was a good idea."

He seemed mollified at least. "You want a copy to jerk off to?"

I rolled my eyes and smiled genuinely this time. "Uh, no, I'm good thanks. It was hot, though. The boy underwear might get requested a lot though. You might need to buy some more."

His eyes lit up. "I wonder if I can sell the pairs with my jizz on them?"

"Jesus Christ." Then I thought about it. "Probably, and for a lot of money."

He pulled out his phone. "I'm gonna search that up."

My god.

"When are you doing your first video?" he asked, still thumbing his phone screen.

"Probably tonight," I replied. "I guess."

I wasn't sure how this was our life now, but it sure beat working the street.

"Oh, Benji said he'll come over tomorrow," Fitch said. He looked up at me and smiled. "Said he's gonna try and do two videos in one day. Ambitious or horny, I dunno."

"Both," I allowed.

He chuckled. "He was gonna try doing a jerk-off scene in the bathroom at Nolan's place, just on his phone. Kinda hard when he's not here to do them all the time."

He shrugged. "Dunno what the lighting situation is like in Nolan's bathroom though."

"Maybe we can edit the lighting," I suggested. "It's a good idea to have some different locations. Certainly couldn't hurt. As long as there's nothing identifiable anywhere to give Nolan or his house away."

Fitch's smile brightened. "I love that this is our life now."

"Don't miss working the street?"

"You mean, do I miss random grotty strangers with dick cheese? Uh, that'd be a very hard no."

I made a face. "Ew."

He shrugged. "Well, we gotta get this channel up and running asap or I will be back working the street with random grotty strangers—"

I put my hand up. "Please don't say dick cheese again. Like, ever."

He laughed and headed toward his room. "Okay, I need to call Dom about the likelihood of selling my jizz-crusty underwear. And maybe do a solo jerk-off scene. Who woulda thought watching my own porn videos would be so fucking hot."

His room door closed, and I stood there, wondering how, as Fitch had said, this was my life now. After all the shit I'd been through, all the terrible things, and now I had friends like Fitch who could talk so openly about sex and life, I was living authentically, and despite every-thing, I was happy. I had begun opening up to Fitch and Benji more lately, because I loved them like brothers and best friends. I needed them, their support, and their unconditional love for me.

When we'd agreed to do the online sex channel, I made the decision to be my authentic self. It wasn't just for kink ratings or because there was a market for it. I'd done it for me.

I'd ordered new butt plugs and some cute little frilly skirts and lacey knickers. I expected Fitch and Benji to make a fuss. But they'd both seen them and they'd not even cared. Actually, Fitch had picked up the skirt and, meeting my eyes, he'd said, "Well this is hot as fuck."

No judgement. No jokes, no sneers. No negativity. Only acceptance.

Fifteen-year-old me would have never dreamed living this life right now was possible.

I needed to remind myself of that more often.

I turned the screen off and smiled, then set about prepping for my first video.

IT WAS EASIER than I thought it would be. Actually, it was no different to what I did at Leon and Marek's house; I was clean, moisturised, lubed up. I painted my nails hot pink. I chose the prettiest pink frilly mini skirt that didn't even reach the tops of my thighs. My panties were white lace with matching suspenders and stockings.

I didn't normally do the stockings but I loved how they felt, and I decided I should take these to Leon and

Marek's on the weekend. I'm sure they'd like them on me . . .

I decided to start with a front-on angle, then move into the side angle Fitch had used. We'd worked out where on the bed to kneel, sit, or lie, depending on where the camera was situated.

I began with my back to the camera, and I slowly knelt on the bed, giving the camera a view of my arse and thighs, the suspenders, stockings, the skirt, the butt plug.

I ran my hands up the backs of my thighs and gave my arse a squeeze, then rattled the butt plug. I moaned and settled into kneeling in the front-facing position. It gave the viewer a great shot of the suspenders on my thighs and if I lifted the skirt just right, when I was skimming my hand over myself, my cock and balls dipped down below the hem of my skirt.

"I need to make sure I'm ready for my daddy," I murmured. "He doesn't like to wait."

Then I picked up the seven-inch pink silicone dildo and drizzled it with lube. I began stroking it as I would a cock, smearing the slickness, giving it a good pump, and moaning as I did.

"Daddy's so big," I said, my pitch high and breathy. Then I knelt up and, lifting my skirt a little, began rubbing the dildo against my own dick. "Daddy's so much bigger than me."

My cock was confined by the panties, though they barely concealed me at all. I let the head of my cock slip out and began to frot with the dildo.

It felt so fucking good. I felt awkward speaking to no

one, speaking for the viewers. Fitch had made it look so easy. He was a natural, talking and whimpering like he did. He made it sound as if Dominic was in the room with him . . .

And that gave me an idea.

Pretend Leon and Marek were here. Pretend as if they were doing this to me, or if I was doing this for them, at least.

So that's what I did.

I tried to be mindful of the camera, of the angles, but I closed my eyes and imagined Leon and Marek were with me. My hands were Marek's, the dildo was Leon, my whispers and moans were for them.

I could hear them in my head. Things they'd said to me, the way they murmured that I was such a good boy, the way they held me, reassured me, made me feel safe and loved.

"Yes, daddy," I cried out as the dildo was fully seated inside me. I rocked back and forth, feeling every inch, just how Leon loved it. Marek's arms would wrap around me, their soft kisses on my head, on my neck . . . "You make me feel so good."

I was lost to it after that.

Imagining it was them. Wishing it was.

I felt their absence when it was over, a hollow satisfaction when I opened my eyes and remembered that I was alone.

I'd made myself come to visions of them. It was intense and felt far too real.

Just like their absence.

God, I needed them. I needed their strength and comfort. I needed the way they replaced my troubles with a heady bubble of adoration and need.

But I wasn't due to see them for two more nights.

Two nights may as well have been forever.

I cleaned myself up, the bed and all the toys I'd used, and changed into some shorts and a T-shirt before watching my video to see if it was usable.

All while pretending my heart didn't ache, that I wasn't missing Leon and Marek like crazy.

A quiet knock at my door made me realise I'd zoned out, the video almost finished, and I couldn't remember watching any of it.

Fitch stuck his head in. "Hey. How'd you go?"

"Oh," I said, sitting up, trying to shake off this heavy funk. "Kinda tuned out. Is it awkward to watch your own stuff?"

He came in, concern in his eyes, and sat on the end of my bed. "Everything okay?"

I sighed, mad at myself for letting my emotions show. "Yeah. I just . . . I dunno . . ."

He sat patiently, not saying a thing—which was not something Fitch usually did—while he waited for me to continue.

"I wasn't kinda feeling it," I said. "So I kinda pretended I wasn't alone . . ." I swallowed hard. "That I was with . . . them."

"Your daddies?"

I nodded. "It made it so much easier. It was hot, even. I was caught up in make believing it was them . . ."

Goddammit.

"And?" he prompted when I didn't keep talking.

"And when I opened my eyes, they weren't there."

Fitch frowned and let out a long sigh. "Oh man."

I buried my face in my hands. "Stupid, huh? So fucking stupid."

"Ky," Fitch said. Then he gently pulled one of my hands away. "It's not stupid."

"I know better than to get attached. I know it's not real. I know what I am to them," I whispered. "And it is stupid to let myself think otherwise because hope is a dangerous fucking thing."

His whole face was sad, and Fitch was rarely sad. I hated that I'd been the one to make him that way.

"Sorry," I whispered. "Just ignore me. It'll pass. I'm just in a funk or something. I don't even know."

"You're allowed to miss them when you're not with them," he murmured. "You're allowed to miss how they make you feel. That high, that rush, the feeling of being safe and protected. You're allowed to miss that."

Jesus Christ.

"In my head," I admitted, "they were here. Then when I realised they weren't . . ."

I sighed.

"Call them," he said. "If you can't see them, then talk to them. Surely that's allowed."

"Allowed?"

"Yeah, in your contract."

I'd forgotten I'd told him about that . . .

"Is being their boy only for times you're with them?

Because that sounds like it's just for their benefit, not yours."

I tried not to get defensive because what Fitch was saying came from a good place, and it was kinda true.

"There are no rules about stuff like that. It's more about confidentiality."

"Then call them. Tell them you need to hear your daddies' voices before bed tonight. They'll love that shit."

I snorted at the ridiculousness. "Maybe."

Fitch nodded sagely. "We have to understand how the daddy mind works. They might not need us all the time, but a boy always needs a daddy, and if you tell them that—if you pout and be all sad and look up at them through your lashes with sad puppy eyes—they will give in, one hundred percent of the time."

I laughed at that. "Manipulation 101 classes by Professor Fitch."

He grinned at me. "Is it manipulation though? Or all part of the game we play?"

I thought about that for a second. "I don't even know if I'm playing a game here."

"Okay, so wrong word choice by me. Is it manipulation? Or all part of the *role* we play?"

That was better . . . somewhat.

He patted my leg. "Call them. Message them. Whatever. Just contact them. Are they even in town?"

"I think so."

I hadn't heard anything to the contrary but that was also part of the issue. They had no reason to tell me shit unless it affected our planned days together.

Before I could dive headfirst into that spiral, Fitch nodded to the camera. "Can I see your video? Or are you still working on it?"

I looked at the screen, the image of me wearing the pink skirt, sitting on a dildo frozen, right where I'd paused it.

"I, uh, I haven't watched it yet," I said. "I don't even remember filming the end of it, I was so caught up in my own head. Once I watch it through and make sure I don't say any names or anything, then you'll be the first to watch it, okay?"

"Deal. And if it's really hot, it's going straight to the spank bank."

I snorted. "You're such a whore."

He preened. "Thanks." Then he nodded to the screen again. "That skirt is fucking hot, just so you know. If you want to wear that around the apartment because you like it, then fucking wear it."

I felt my face heat and my heart felt a rush of warmth too. "Thanks," I whispered. "I do like it."

"Then wear it! Those short little tiered skirts are too cute to be hidden away. And your arse and thighs? Ky, baby, you need to flaunt that shit."

I was embarrassed, while my chest ached with warmth and acceptance. "Thank you." My nose burned and I had to blink back tears.

Fitch grabbed my hand. "Oh my god, don't you dare cry. If you cry, then I will cry and I probably won't be able to stop, and we'll be two sobbing, snotty queers for hours and you'll make my face all puffy."

I snorted back a teary laugh. His grip on my hand never lessened and, dear god, I needed it. "I don't know why I'm so emotional today."

He gasped. "Are you pregnant? Should I get you some ice cream?"

I rolled my eyes. "I dunno, can arse-babies be a thing?"

Fitch laughed and patted his belly. "Not sure, but I will keep taking Dom's loads, for the sake of science."

"Yeah. Science."

We were both quiet for a second and I took in a deep breath and let it out slowly. Maybe I needed to offload some of this weight, this burden I'd carried for so long. "I always liked wearing skirts," I whispered. "Playing dress-up when I was three years old, I had to wear the Cinderella dress. I'd sleep in it and my parents just thought it was a toddler thing. I idolised my older sister so . . ."

I sighed heavily and Fitch waited patiently, still holding my hand.

"But as I got older, those dresses didn't fit me anymore, but god, I wanted them to. I love the feel of it. It makes me feel . . . pretty." I made a face. "My parents always called my sister pretty and they fussed over her. Their perfect golden child, and I wanted that. I would take her skirts out of the laundry hamper and wear them with nothing else. I'd keep the bathroom door locked and I'd pretend to be pretty like her. God, I just love how it feels. It makes me feel . . ."

I was going to say pretty again but stopped myself.

"Empowered?" Fitch supplied.

My gaze shot to his. "Yes."

Holy shit. He understood?

"Yes. Empowered, and a bit naughty and a lot pretty, and I don't know why . . ." I sighed out a laugh. "I don't want to be a girl. I'm not a girl. I never felt I was female. I never wished I was. It's not like that. It's just femboy stuff."

"You like wearing skirts."

I nodded. "And painting my nails, and sometimes I'll wear some make-up to feel extra special. And my daddies love it. It makes them wild. I'll wear pretty skirts and they make such a fuss. They call me princess and they're so gentle and kind . . ."

I wasn't supposed to be saying this shit.

"Please tell me they rail you so fucking thoroughly while you're wearing a skirt," Fitch said, squeezing my hand. "Like, that is seriously the hottest fucking thing I've ever heard."

I laughed, embarrassed and relieved and yet, still my chest ached . . .

"Oh my god, they do," Fitch mumbled. "What did you say before? One holds you while the other fucks you? While you're wearing a skirt?"

I mimicked locking my lips with a key and throwing it away.

"That's a yes. Jesus, Ky. That's going straight into my spank bank."

"Gross."

"I'm one hundred percent going to tell Dom to buy me a cheerleading skirt to go with my football crop top."

"You are such a whore."

He seemed genuinely pleased, pulled out his phone, and shot Dom a quick text. I didn't need to read the screen to know he was putting in the request. He hit Send and did a little butt wiggle on my bed, and his phone rang a second later. He squealed as he answered.

I could hear Dom's deep rumble of a voice, and whatever he said made Fitch laugh. He stood up and turned to me. "One second, daddy," he said into the phone before pressing it to his chest. Then he bent down and kissed my forehead. "Love you, Ky. Thank you for telling me."

His words burned something in me, making the ache in my chest worse.

"You need to call them," Fitch whispered. "Now, Ky. Call them now."

He left my room, his phone back to his ear, and I was left alone with his instruction and deep sense of longing.

I took my phone, found Marek's number, my thumb hovering over the Call button.

I'd never done this before. I'd never initiated contact or even called them for anything other than things like locations or pick-up times.

But I'd never felt like this, either.

Not since I was lost and alone, barely nineteen, and homeless.

Fuck the ache in my chest was burning now.

I needed them, and what Fitch said was right. I

should be able to call them when I needed them, not just when they wanted me.

I opted for Marek first because he was the soft-hearted one, the tender one, caring and gentle.

My god, I needed him.

I hit Call, my heart hammering, fully expecting it to go through to voicemail. But even hearing his voice would make me feel better . . .

But the call answered and it wasn't Marek's voice I heard. It was Leon.

"Kylan," he said. His big gruff voice felt like his warm arms wrapping around me, and it pulled a soft sob out of my lungs, and I burst into tears.

"Daddy."

FOUR
LEON ELLINGTON

I HADN'T BEEN EXPECTING to feel such things.

Marek and I had just walked through the door, and he'd gone back to the car to get his suit bag we'd collected from the dry cleaner. His phone was on the kitchen counter, and I was making him a pot of tea when his phone rang.

Normally I wouldn't care, wouldn't even look, but it was sitting face up and Kylan's name caught my eye.

Hmm. That's odd . . .

"Kylan's calling you," I yelled out.

"Then answer it, darling," Marek replied.

I picked up the phone and hit Answer just as Marek slid the suit bag over the back of the sofa. He was watching me, concerned too, because our boy simply didn't call us. Texted occasionally, but call?

Never.

"Kylan," I said.

I heard his breath catch and a quiet sob that struck fear into me. Then his broken, "Daddy."

"Kylan, baby, what's wrong?" I demanded.

Marek rushed over to me, his hand on my chest, his eyes wide with worry.

Kylan cried, his words barely distinguishable between his sobs. "I'm sorry. Nothing, I just . . . I don't even know."

"Where are you?" I demanded. "We're on our way. We're coming to you."

Marek already had the keys and we were in the car before I realised Kylan hadn't answered.

"Kylan," I demanded.

"I'm at home," he said, still crying. "I'm so sorry. I just needed to hear your voice."

"He's at his place," I mumbled to Marek. Then I spoke into the phone. "Okay, Ky, baby, stay on the phone. We're on our way."

My mind ran with a thousand possibilities.

Had someone hurt him? Was he okay? What had they done to him?

Thank god Marek was driving because fear and rage were not a safe combination.

I was scared for him. And if someone had hurt him?

I would fucking kill them.

Marek's hand slid onto my thigh and squeezed, as if he could sense my anger, my fear.

My concern.

Our sweet princess was crying, and it was killing me that I wasn't there.

That I hadn't been able to protect him.

See, that's the thing. I prided myself on taking care of my boys. Marek, first and foremost, always. But then Kylan had come into our lives. What was supposed to be a fun interlude had become a regular thing, then a permanent thing.

An important thing.

I was their provider, their protector.

I was their daddy.

They were mine.

Mine to look after, mine to care for, mine to keep safe.

Mine to keep.

When we finally turned onto Oxford Street, I spoke into the phone. "Okay, Kylan, we're almost there. Come downstairs. We'll just have to pull up."

"Okay," he replied with a sniffle.

"I'm hanging up now," I said. "See you soon."

"'Kay."

I ended the call and slid Marek's phone into the centre console. "He's really upset," I said. "Crying and sobbing. I couldn't make out what he was saying."

Marek's knuckles on the steering wheel went white, and he glanced between me and the road. His eyes were full of concern as well, and I loved that my husband's emotions mirrored my own. "Is he hurt?"

"I don't know."

Marek let out a low measured breath before he pulled up, earning a blare of a horn from the car behind us. I got out of the car, gave that arsehole driver a glare that made him school his features as he merged into traffic and kept driving.

Just as I opened the back door, Kylan came around the corner, his eyes blotchy and nose red, and his face crumpled when he saw me.

It felt as if I'd been struck with a hot iron through my heart.

I hurried him into the backseat and, surprising myself, followed him in. Unable to bear it another second, I pulled him straight into my lap and held him as he cried.

"My sweet boy," I murmured.

He buried his face into my neck and clung to me. "Daddy."

Marek's eyes in the rear-vision mirror met mine and I frowned at him. Something was definitely wrong.

He didn't seem to have any outwardly visible or physical wounds, but he was very clearly in some kind of pain.

I rubbed Kylan's back and rocked him, soothing him while he cried. "It's okay, baby boy," I whispered. "Your daddies are here now."

Marek smiled at me in the rear-vision mirror.

Kylan sobbed, then tried to calm himself. "I'm sorry," he said, over and over. "I never meant to be a problem."

"You're no problem," I murmured.

"You're both so good to me, and I just . . ." He began to cry again, and I realised that talking in the car was pointless. He needed nothing but comfort and reassurance now. Talking could wait.

"Shh," I said, kissing the top of his head. "You can tell us later. Just let daddy hold you."

He snuggled in, fisting my shirt. "Thank you, daddy. Thank you so much."

He'd stopped crying by the time we got home. I helped him inside, and when Marek had offered his embrace on the sofa, Kylan climbed into his lap much like he'd been in mine in the car. Curled into the smallest ball possible, his head on Marek's neck.

Marek's sad eyes met mine over Kylan's head. I sat down next to them and rubbed Kylan's back. "You're okay now," I said softly.

"I feel so foolish," Kylan said. "I don't want you to be mad at me."

"Mad at you?" Marek asked. "Why would we be mad? Did something happen?"

Kylan sniffled. "I've been a mess all day. I don't know why. And I was missing you both so much. Even though it's not my day to be with you. I'm sorry. But I was upset at home and Fitch said I should call you, and I didn't want to because I didn't want to be a bother, and I didn't expect you to come over. I just needed to hear your voices."

Oh, this poor boy.

I leaned in, cuddling him but also Marek as well. "You scared me," I admitted. "I was so worried. I thought someone had hurt you."

Kylan turned his head so he could see me. "I'm sorry. I didn't mean to make you worry."

"Of course we would worry," Marek cooed, stroking

Kylan's hair, the side of his face. "How could we not worry?"

"I wasn't sure if I could call," he said. "I never have before, but it's not stipulated in our contract that I can't call, so I thought . . . I just needed to hear your voices. I'm so sorry."

"Fitch told you to call us?" I asked as softly as I could.

Ky nodded. "I told him I missed you both so much and I needed your arms around me so bad I could almost feel you. Then it made my missing you so much worse."

"Oh, baby," Marek murmured.

"And Fitch said if I couldn't call you when I needed you this bad, then it wasn't fair. He said a daddy might not need his boy every day, but a boy needs his daddies all the time, and then he said I should call you because you'd both understand."

Marek smiled at me over Kylan's head now as he rocked him a little. "Of course we understand. You can call us anytime you need."

Kylan sniffled again. "I don't deserve you. But I'd be so lost without you."

I gave him a squeeze, kissing the back of his head. "You do deserve us."

There was something else, something he wasn't telling us. And the more I thought about it, the more I realised it was maybe because he didn't know.

"You know what I think?" I began. "Sit up, Kylan, and look at us."

He did as I asked, sitting between us on the sofa, his

hands in his lap, fidgeting nervously. His face was a streaky, puffy mess, and it hurt my heart.

I took his hand. "You're not in trouble. In fact, I'm pleased you called when you needed us."

He looked up at me, eyes wide. "You are?"

"Of course. What Fitch said is correct. A boy needs his daddies all the time."

Ky nodded. "But I've never felt like I did today before."

"And you feel better now?" I asked.

He nodded eagerly. "Much."

I smiled for him. "Hmm. Kylan, I wonder if you were feeling all out of sorts today because you felt unsafe."

His eyes met mine, big and wide. "Unsafe?"

I gave him a nod. "Did something happen today? Something that made you need reassurance?"

His eyes welled with tears, and as soon as one spilled over, he scrubbed it away.

"I did my first solo video today," he said, voice timid. "Fitch and Benji did theirs and had no problem, but I . . ." he shuddered as if his skin didn't fit properly. "I wasn't feeling it, and then I tried to imagine I was with you."

"Me?" I asked.

He baulked and blinked in surprise. "No. Both of you. Always both of you."

I slid my hand over his and squeezed, my heart full.

Marek gave me a smile. "Go on, Kylan. You imagined you were with us?"

He nodded. "And then I relaxed, and it felt so real. I imagined you both holding me; Marek's arms and hands, and Leon's . . ." His eyes met mine. "I imagined the dildo was you, daddy. And I got so into it. It was so easy then, but then it was over and I opened my eyes and I was alone and—" He put his palm to his sternum. "I felt hollowed out and empty and alone, and I needed you both so bad. And I realised then—" He sniffled and wiped away another tear. "That I always will be."

"Always will be what, sweet boy?" Marek murmured.

"Alone."

What?

"No," I whispered. "You're not alone. You have us, and you have great friends who love you very much."

"They'll leave me," he whispered. "Benji's living with Nolan now, and it'll only be a matter of time before Fitch goes. They're all I have. I don't know what I'll do without them. I'm trying to be more open with them so they know I care, but it will only make it hurt worse in the end."

The resignation in his quiet voice, the sadness on his beautiful face, his silent tears . . .

It caused me physical pain.

I pulled him and Marek into my arms, almost crushing Kylan between us. "You're okay," I murmured. "Sweet, sweet boy."

"You're safe here," Marek told him.

And that was just it though. He was safe here, while he was here, he had the both of us to meet every need he had.

But when he wasn't here?

"You were worried about where you fit in," I said gently. "Worried about how things are changing and wondering where that leaves you. Feeling unsettled and adrift and unsafe."

He nodded and sniffled. "Yes. Yes, daddy. That's exactly it. I've been alone so long, and then I'm finally not, and now I feel like I'm losing it all again. I hate it."

Marek frowned at me over the top of Ky's head. "What can we do, baby? What can we do to make you feel better?"

"You already have," he replied. "Being here with you, like this. I feel better already. I'm sorry to be a burden . . ."

A burden . . .

That word rankled something in me, igniting an anger I hadn't felt in a long time. I pulled back, and with my hand under his chin, I made him look at me. "Listen to me, Kylan. You are not a burden. Don't ever think you are, and don't ever call yourself that again."

Kylan's lip trembled, his eyes wide. "I'm sorry."

Now he thought I was mad at him.

I pressed a soft kiss to his lips. "You're not in trouble," I reassured him. "I just don't want to hear you calling someone we care about a burden, okay?"

It took him a second to realise I was talking about him. "Me?"

Marek chuckled. "Yes, princess. Of course we care about you."

And we did.

Very much. He had become an important part of our lives. We both adored him.

Kylan wiggled back so he could see both our faces. Fresh tears welled in his eyes. "You care about me?"

Marek put a gentle hand to his cheek. "How could we not?"

Then Kylan let out a teary laugh and threw his arms around both our necks and hugged us. "Thank you, thank you. I promise I'll be the best boy you could ever want. I'll make you happy, I promise."

I rubbed his back. "You already do make us happy."

He leaned back, his bony arse on my thigh bone. I picked him up and repositioned him. "Oh, sorry," he said with an awkward smile. But then he looked up at me with big adoring eyes and my heart melted all over again for him. "Thank you, daddy. For explaining what I couldn't. And you too, daddy," he said, looking at Marek. "For coming to get me. I'm sorry if I made you worry."

"Do you feel better now, princess?" Marek asked him.

Kylan nodded. "Yes. You always make me feel better. Sometimes I get all up in my head and normally I'm okay, but today I couldn't shake it. Fitch was right. I needed you both, and you both came to get me. I'm sorry if you were busy or at work. I don't even know what time it is."

"It's dinner time," I said. "How about we cook you something and you can tell us about the video you made?"

He blushed. "Oh. Okay."

Marek ran his thumb over Kylan's heated cheek. He loved the way Kylan flushed. "Did you want to go have a shower? Dinner will be done by the time you come out, then we can eat and go to bed."

Kylan looked surprised. "I didn't think I was staying. It's not one of my two nights—"

I put my finger to his lips. "Did you want to stay, boy? It can be an additional night this week if you need it."

He nodded eagerly. "Yes, daddy. You don't need to pay me extra. Just being here is enough. And I can walk home from here in the morning, you don't need to drive me anywhere. I won't be any trouble, I promise."

"You're never any trouble," I said, helping him off my lap. "Now, go be a good boy and have a shower before dinner."

He nodded again and I watched him as he skittered out of the room before I turned to Marek. He was looking at me, as I knew he would be.

"We need to talk," I whispered.

Marek nodded. "We do." He sighed. "That poor sweet boy. How can we reassure him any more than we already have? I thought he felt secure with us, but clearly not."

The truth was, I thought we had reassured him enough as well, but something was lacking somewhere.

"His fear of abandonment doesn't stem from us," I said gently. "But we need to work harder at reminding him we're not going anywhere. You're still one hundred percent happy with this arrangement?"

Marek nodded. "Very happy, darling."

"Same," I admitted.

"I saw how worried you were," Marek said fondly. "You care about him, deeply."

I sighed. "I do. And I know you do too." I brushed my thumb along Marek's jaw. "I thought someone had hurt him and I was about to rain down an unholy firestorm . . ."

Marek leaned in and kissed me softly. "You are such a sweet man. A good man. But someone somewhere along that poor boy's life did hurt him, and we need to tread very carefully."

I nodded. "Agreed."

"Everything you said to him was spot on. He was feeling unsafe and uncertain. He's afraid of change and he's petrified of being abandoned."

"Again."

Marek's smile was sad. "But he has us now, and we have no plans to terminate our contract with him, do we?"

"No. None. If you're happy to continue, then I am as well."

"Oh, I'm very happy to continue."

"As am I."

Marek put his hand to my cheek. "You're so good with him. I hope you know how much I love seeing you with him. How you care for him, tend to him, protect him. It makes me very happy, Leon."

I leaned in and kissed him. "Ditto, my love."

Marek preened a little, then clapped his hands on his thighs and stood up. "Well, he knows he can call us now. Hopefully he's reassured and content. Though we should start dinner to feed him before we put him to bed."

I followed him into the kitchen. "So, tonight should be more about reassurance and security, yes? No sex, just cuddling, to make sure he knows he's safe, right? So we're on the same page when he comes back downstairs."

Marek chuckled as he took a container from the fridge. "I think so, yes. I think he needs that from us tonight."

Okay, good.

As long as Marek and I were on the same page, everything would be fine. From the very beginning, we'd always been very open about our needs when we played with a third person.

And we were very open about how excited we were when we first met Kylan, and we had long conversations when we considered inviting him into a more permanent situation.

We both saw something special in him.

We were both attracted to him, but it was more than just sexual fantasies and desires. We both wanted to wrap him up with affection and praise, and we wanted him to thrive.

We both wanted a young man to fawn over, to pamper and spoil. To wear his pretty femboy outfits and moan and whimper while we took turns fucking him.

We wanted a boy who wanted all that as much as we did.

And we found that in Kylan.

But tonight was a good reminder that it wasn't only

about sex. It was never just about sex, and it should never be just about sex.

It was a daddy's responsibility to meet all the needs of his boy, and that meant emotional needs as well.

And being the emotional support pillars he so clearly needed tonight was a proud moment for me—for me as Marek's husband, and for the daddy in me. It made me feel worthy.

It validated the part of me that craved to be Kylan's daddy.

It felt as if we'd cemented something in our relationship tonight, making us stronger, better.

Not just mine and Marek's, but with Kylan. Our *agreement* felt greater and in a lot of ways clearer.

This was who I was meant to be.

And this was who Marek was meant to be. Both of us, together.

As I was finishing setting the table, carrying the salad bowl, I stopped to give Marek a kiss on the cheek. "I love you," I murmured.

He paused at the grill to smile at me. "And I am the luckiest man on the planet."

There was a quiet sigh behind us, and we turned to find Kylan standing there, timid and perhaps even embarrassed. His hair was washed and brushed neatly, his skin looked scrubbed, rosy and fresh. He even wore a bare touch of lip balm, but the pièce de résistance was his pyjamas.

A pretty pink nightie, soft fabric that clung to his body. It barely covered his panties, and he knew

—oh, he knew all too well—that it was a favourite of ours.

He was stunning.

And did I say no sex tonight?

I regretted that with a quiet, tortured groan.

Before Kylan could become confused, Marek held his hand out. "Come here, sweet boy. You look radiant."

Kylan glided toward him, taking his hand. "Thank you, daddy."

Marek slid his arm around Kylan's tiny waist. "The salmon's almost done. Is that okay with you, darling?"

Kylan nodded. "Very. Can I do anything to help?"

Marek kissed his temple. "No. We are looking after you tonight. Anything you want, just name it."

Kylan's wide eyes went to Marek, then to me. "Anything?"

I groaned again, and this time Kylan frowned. But Marek laughed and gave him a squeeze. "I think daddy's torturing himself over there," Marek said with a fond smile in my direction. "He said no sex tonight, but then you came down wearing this, looking just delicious."

Kylan's cheeks flushed and he melted into Marek a little, but he gave me his big puppy eyes. "No sex tonight? Did I . . . am I in trouble?"

I couldn't help but chuckle as I went to him, lifted his chin, and pressed a soft kiss to his lips. "No, princess. Of course not. I just thought a night of cuddles in bed, maybe a movie, might be what you need tonight."

He looked adorably sad for half a second before he nodded. "It does sound nice." Then he looked down at his pretty pyjamas. "Should I change into something else?"

I lightly tapped my finger to his nose. "Don't change a thing."

"Okay, dinner's served," Marek said, the expertly cooked salmon now on our plates on the table. He pulled out Kylan's chair. "Come take a seat, sweetheart. Can I get you anything else?"

Kylan sat down eloquently and waited for us to sit, Marek to his right, me to his left at the head of the table. "No thank you, daddy," he said, looking at Marek as if he hung the moon. "I have everything I need right here."

The way Marek looked at him, then at me, smiling and proud . . . made my heart so fucking happy.

These two made me so happy.

Could I have both of them in my bed and not indulge a little?

I was going to have to.

Surely, I could control myself for one night. Surely.

Even after Kylan helped clean up after dinner, poking his pert little arse out more than he had to, showing off his half-hard boy-dick in those too-small panties.

It was a measure of self-control for me. Marek, on the other hand, seemed to find it funny, the way Kylan teased and how I had to close my eyes and count to ten several times.

Getting into bed with aching balls was not helping either. Kylan snuggling in between us, propped up on the pillows against the headboard so he could watch TV.

How he smiled so genuinely, so innocently, it tempered my fires a little.

He did need this. Nothing but reassurance and protection to feel safe and happy.

So while my sexual fire was unlit, my heart burned more than enough to sustain me. This was, perhaps, the daddiest thing we'd ever done with him, for him.

"Are you happy now, boy?" I asked him.

He nodded earnestly. "Oh yes, daddy," he whispered, snuggling down the bed a little. "Between you both is where I'm happiest."

"Are you sleepy?" Marek asked gently.

Kylan nodded. "Yes, daddy."

He opened his arms for him and Kylan snuggled in, his head on Marek's chest.

I leaned over and kissed Marek's cheek, then Kylan's head. "Sweet dreams."

I turned the TV off and settled down, just to lie there and watch them. These perfect two. The way Kylan fit so perfectly against him, the way Marek held him, and the way he smiled at me over the top of Kylan's head.

Even in the dark, as Kylan slept, I could make out Marek's face; his moustache, his eyes looking right back at me, his soft smile.

"I love you," I mouthed.

His smile widened and he tightened his arm around Kylan. "Love you too," he murmured.

I put my arm over Kylan's waist, my hand on Marek's arm, relishing the touch of my two men, and closed my eyes.

Content and happy in ways I couldn't begin to describe, and a peaceful sleep came way too easily.

I WOKE to Marek and Kylan standing beside Marek's side of the bed. "Whassup?" I croaked, no clue what was wrong or what time it was. It didn't look too light outside yet. "What's wrong?"

Marek held up the covers. "Nothing. I just caught this little one in the shower."

Kylan giggled as he scampered into the bed. He came right over to me, wiggling and happy. He was shower-warm and smelled fresh. I kept my hand on his hip to keep him from wiggling against my cock.

Sleeping next to him while he was wearing that cute little nightie and brief set had been the very best torture.

Normally we'd fall asleep all fucked out. Sometimes my balls were so drained I couldn't have gone another round in the morning if I'd wanted to.

But last night? There'd been no release. Hell, it'd been three days since my last orgasm. My cock was more than awake and eager now . . .

"What were you doing in the shower, princess?" I asked, though I was confident I knew exactly what he was doing . . . At least I hoped I was right.

"I was making sure I was ready for you, daddy," he said, his big eyes bright and innocent.

Oh, hell yes.

My balls drew down, my cock pulsing in response. "Is that right, boy?"

He nodded. "I slept so well that I woke up early, and I know you both have to go to work this morning, so I wanted to make sure you went to work happy."

"I heard the shower," Marek said. "He was just finishing up when I went in."

Kylan looked back at Marek. "You said I did a good job."

"Very thorough," Marek replied.

I chuckled and Kylan beamed up at me. He loved praise, and he loved to make us proud. He was so radiant when he was well cared for. "I know tonight's technically my night," Kylan said, "but I really want to make you happy, daddy. As happy as you make me."

I put my hand to his cheek, thumbing his lip. "Is that right, princess? How happy is that?"

He nodded eagerly. "So happy," he breathed. His chest rose and fell, his eyes got bigger. "Please, daddy." He ran his hand over my chest and wiggled in closer, determined to feel my cock. "I'm ready for you, daddy. I need it. I need you both."

Christ.

"You need it, huh?"

He nodded again, though there was urgency in his eyes, in his tone. "Need my daddies so bad. Take turns with me. Do what you want with me, daddy. Anything. Please."

I grunted.

Those were dangerous fucking words.

"Need daddy's cock," Kylan whimpered. "Need daddy's come."

I shot up, and pinning Kylan face down on the bed, I straddled his small hips. Marek handed me the lube and leaned against the headboard to watch.

To wait for his turn.

"He's a needy boy today," I said, sliding Kylan's nightie up so I could peel his panties down, revealing his pale cheeks. "Look at this perfect little arse."

So perfect. So delicious.

Kylan tried to rise up for me, but he was no match for my weight, my size. I kept him pinned right where I wanted him.

My cock felt thick and heavy, desperate to sink into him. There would be no stamina required for this. It was gonna be fast, hard, and deep.

"Don't be too needy, boy," I warned. "Daddy doesn't want to hurt you. Gotta get you ready for me first."

I popped the lid and drizzled some lube down his crack, and he fisted the pillow, stretching his back.

Desperate.

Keeping his legs together, I worked my thumb down his slit, dipping my thumb tip into his hole, more and more with each pass.

"You were a good boy to get yourself ready for me." I praised him, voice low and rough. "You knew how you teased daddy wearing this pretty nightie to bed. I wanted you all night."

"Yes, daddy," he said, voice tight with frustration, still trying to raise his arse and spread his legs to take more of my thumb. He whined out a desperate sob. "I wanted you all night too. So bad, daddy. I need you both so bad."

Marek stroked Kylan's hair. "Don't cry, sweetheart. We'll give you what you need."

"Hmm," I said. "I think he needs his pacifier. Does our sweet princess want his pacifier?"

He raised his head, nodding. "Oh yes, please."

Marek grinned at me and I gave Kylan some room to move. He slid over to lie between Marek's legs and pulled at Marek's pyjama pants, eagerly taking Marek's cock into his mouth.

Marek's hips flexed and his expression was one of exquisite torture. I was so turned on, so ready to be inside Kylan, I couldn't wait another second.

"Oh, good boy," I cooed, pulling the front of my pants down and slicking my cock with lube. Then, still with Kylan's legs together, I pressed my cock into his slick crack. I felt the resistance of his hole and, leaning forward, pushed through.

Kylan choked on Marek's cock, pulling off so he could cry out and catch his breath. I sank all the way in, down to my balls. Such sweet tight heat that ripped a groan of pleasure from my lungs.

"Daddy," he wailed, pushing up on his hands, squeezing his arse around me.

I gripped his hair and pulled his head back, directing him back onto Marek's cock. "Take your pacifier, princess. Suck it real good."

He did, his head bobbing up and down on Marek

while I slowly fucked his arse, his body between us, pale and petite.

Perfect.

Marek's eyes met mine, heavy lidded, full of desire. "Love watching you fuck him," he said. Then he hissed, his fingers finding Kylan's hair, tugging gently. "Fuck, this is good."

My pace quickened, too turned on, too far gone to do anything but fuck. My orgasm was coming at me like a freight train and I drove into Kylan, over and over, needing the release.

"Daddy's gonna come," I bit out, slamming into Kylan one last time. My cock was so hard, my balls drew up and the dam of pleasure burst. I came so hard, driving into him so deep he took Marek into his throat as he took my come.

I groaned loud and long with each pulse, with each wave of ecstasy. White-hot fire ripped through me, my brain spun, and I could barely register Marek's moan, his face of pure bliss as he came after me.

I wanted to stay inside Kylan forever.

I wanted to collapse on top of him but was reluctant to hurt him.

I kissed his spine, his nape, the back of his head. "This sweet boy, what a good boy he is."

Marek's glazed-over eyes met mine and he chuckled. "Damn."

I pulled out slowly, reluctantly. My heavy cock slipping free. "Want to feel how sweet he is?" I asked.

Marek nodded, and extracting himself from under

Kylan, he swapped places with me. He pulled Kylan up onto his knees, put his half-hard dick to Kylan's open hole, and slid into him. He took Kylan's hips and sank all the way in, and Kylan cried out. "Oh, daddy, yes, yes."

I lifted Kylan's chin, drawing him up to meet my eyes. "I want to taste my husband," I said before crashing my mouth to his. He took my tongue eagerly, his hands on my chest while Marek slow-fucked his used hole.

I reached down to Kylan's cock and began to stroke him. He cried out into my mouth, his little body jerking between us. He was leaking precome, his shaft was slick in my fist.

"Be a good boy and come for me," I said. I moved closer, pressing him between us the way he loved. Marek was still slow fucking him. "Keep going, baby. He's close."

So Marek fucked him harder, and a few thrusts later, Kylan's whole body went rigid, and he cried out as he came.

His semen splashed over me, hot and welcome. He shuddered and whined, clinging to me, and twitching as his orgasm subsided. Then he sagged between us, exhausted and spent.

Marek slipped out of him and I collected Kylan into my arms. "Oh, princess," I soothed. "You did such a good job."

Though Marek's cock was still half-hard. "Got more come for him?" I slid my hand down to Kylan's arse, giving him a wiggle. "He'll take it."

Marek groaned but shook his head. "I could fuck him

all day. If I don't stop now, I will do just that. Maybe we should save it for tonight?"

I looked down at the boy in my arms, his sleepy, smiling face against my chest. "Will you want more tonight, boy?"

I wasn't sure if him staying last night affected our schedule, but hell yes, I wanted him again tonight. Honestly, every night still wouldn't be enough.

"Oh yes please, daddy," he murmured. "All night. Both of you, all night long."

Oh this perfect boy.

He had come into our lives no more than a whim of sexual fantasy to be shared between Marek and myself. A bit of fun, one night of incredible sex.

And now he was a regular feature in our bed. A permanent feature, two nights a week.

Three nights this week. Four, even.

And it still wasn't enough.

Marek and I were in total agreement. Kylan held a place in our hearts.

I gave him a squeeze and pressed a kiss to his fore-head. "Anything you want, princess."

Marek kissed my lips, then Kylan's head. "Anything at all."

FIVE
KYLAN

"WELL, YOU LOOK HAPPIER TODAY," Fitch said, sitting up as I came in. He was watching the TV, but he turned it off when he saw me. "Good night, I take it?"

I fell onto the sofa beside him, acknowledging the ache in my arse as a sweet reminder. "Good night, good morning."

He laughed and nudged me. "You gotta give me something more than that, my guy. You know how I love me some filthy details."

I snorted. "Because you're a whore."

He grinned. "The whoriest whore in all the lands. What did they do to you? Take turns again or a little dabble in the double . . ."

I cleared my throat. "I'm not at liberty to say, but that spit-roast on the menu before breakfast was delicious."

He cracked up laughing giving me a hug. "You lucky fucker. So tell me, who's your favourite?"

I looked at him, horrified. How could I ever choose? "Favourite?"

"Yeah. You gotta like one over the other, right? Even just a smidge."

"Not at all. Both of them equally. And together. Always."

"You never had them one on one if one of them was out of town?"

I shook my head. "It would feel weird. And they're never apart. Like, ever."

He sighed. "How sweet. And hot. So," he said, changing tone. "That spit-roast. Love me some details on that. Was it . . . extra juicy? Succulent, even? When you say delicious, just how good was it?"

I laughed and nudged him with my elbow. "Dee-lish-us."

He sighed dreamily. "I really have to speak to Dom about that replica dildo."

I chuckled. "I'm seeing them tonight again."

He shot me a look. "Three nights this week?"

"Yep. They offered for me to stay at their place all day, but I said no. Their house is nice, don't get me wrong. Like, ridiculously expensive and shit, but I dunno . . . feels wrong without them there. The pool was tempting on my sore arse though."

Fitch's eyes met mine, wide and serious. "They have a pool?"

I nodded. "Oh yeah. Their house? Amazing. Like an art gallery."

"What the fuck are we doing here in this shithole when we could be there?"

I snorted. "Because you aren't supposed to know anything about them, let alone go to their house."

"Well, what are you doing here in this shithole when you could be there?"

I knew he was only joking but his question made me sigh. "Because I'd miss you," I said, quietly and awkwardly. I was sure my face was red, and I wished I could take the words back as soon as I'd said them.

Fitch blinked.

"Don't go making a big deal out—"

He threw his arms around me. "I'd miss you too, Kysie."

I hated that nickname he'd made up. He only used it when he was sulking or sorry. Or stupidly happy, apparently.

I weaselled out of his hold. "Yeah, yeah, okay, let me go."

He put his hands in his lap, but he was jittery with excitement. He could never hide his emotions well. He could never hide anything well.

So I might as well get this over with and done with. In for a penny or whatever that old saying was . . .

"And I wanted to thank you," I added. It was never easy for me to talk about emotions, but I needed to do this. "For telling me to call them. For telling me if they weren't attentive to all my needs, they weren't the real deal."

Fitch smiled and slid his hand over mine. "You talked to them?"

I nodded. "I told them everything I was feeling. Which I never do."

He nodded then. "I know, baby. I know it's hard for you."

"I'm trying to get better at it," I admitted. My heart was hammering so fucking hard. "They said something that kinda hit home, you know, a bit too close to the truth. I guess he would see right through me because he's really smart and just fucking clued-in, ya know?"

"One of your daddies?"

I nodded. "He said yesterday was hard for me because I felt unsafe, and—"

"Unsafe?" Fitch went to instant alert-mode. "Here? With me?"

I snatched up his hand. "No, no. Not like that." I swallowed hard. Having to explain this to him wasn't easy. Leon and Marek just got it, but I was gonna have to admit shit I didn't really want to admit. "Unsafe because things are changing. Benji's living with Nolan now, and you'll be moving in with Dominic soon enough, and that just leaves me. And I'll be alone again. These last two years . . . since I met you and Benj, I . . ."

Fitch squeezed my hand. "Hey. I'm not leaving you. Who said I was moving in with Dom?"

I shrugged. "I just guessed, you know, because you two are so tight, and he clearly loves you. I thought you'd want that. I mean, who wouldn't?" I looked around our shithole unit. "Who'd wanna live here when they could have a luxury house?"

"Me. I wanna live here, with you. Kysie, I don't know what the future holds. None of us do, but I'm not leaving you. Even if, one day down the track, we don't live together anymore, that doesn't mean you're losing me."

I swallowed back tears, determined not to cry again. "Really? You mean that?"

He let go of my hand so he could throw his arms around me. "You can't get rid of me that easy. I'm like a case of herpes. Never really gone no matter how hard you try."

I chuckled, feeling relieved and happy. My heart happy. "Thank you. I, uh . . ."

He pulled back, eyes on mine, waiting. "You what?"

"This isn't easy for me to talk about," I whispered.

"I know."

"I'm trying to get better," I said, letting out a long, measured breath. "At saying shit out loud. Being vulnerable is a hard limit for me."

"A hard limit?" He raised an eyebrow. "One day you're gonna have to tell me what kinky shit you're into."

I smiled despite my mood. Grateful for his ability to make me feel at ease. "I really love you and Benji. You're the only family I have. Like brothers. Horny, perverted brothers, but still . . ."

Fitch laughed. "Okay pot, we kettles have some news for you."

I laughed and threaded our fingers, feeling better

already. "I'm trying to get better at opening up and talking . . . but god." I let out a sigh. "It's not easy for me."

"Because you feel that if you do, if you tell people you love them, they'll leave you."

I nodded, tears welling in my eyes, my heart heavy. He really did understand. "It's easier to pretend nothing matters so when they leave me it doesn't hurt."

Fitch took my hand in both of his. "Oh Kysie, we all feel like that. You, me, and Benji, I'm sure of it. We've been hurt, and it's hard to trust anyone. But you can trust us. Me and Benj, we've got your back. We love you just as you are. However you want to be. You never have to change a single thing, okay?"

I scrubbed away a tear from my cheek. "Thank you. That means a lot to me."

"Like I said to you yesterday, you wanna wear your skirts around the unit, down the street, to a club? Baby, I will hold your hand. Hell, I'll even wear one with you if it will make you feel better."

A teary laugh escaped and more tears fell. "Thank you."

"I'd offer to paint your nails, but you don't want that, trust me. Though I could learn. Bit of practice and who knows."

I cried despite being the happiest I'd felt in far too long. "Thank you." I wiped my cheek again and decided it was time. Time to tell him more about my past. Something I'd not discussed in a long time. "My father found me wearing my sister's skirts, make-up. And he . . ."

Fitch's face fell. "Oh, Ky. I'm sorry."

"He went apeshit. Like, big time."

"He hurt you?"

I nodded. I didn't want to talk about the details or how severe it had been.

"Bad?"

"Bad."

Fitch sighed; his nostrils flared. "I'm sorry, baby. But also fuck him. Fuck him so hard."

I inhaled deeply, trying to shake off the weight of this conversation.

"You deserve to be happy," Fitch said. "We all do. And we deserve to be our true selves."

I nodded. "I know. I'm so grateful for you and Benji. I mean that. I know I don't say that often—"

"Or ever."

I snorted. "I know things are changing, and I want you both to be happy. I'd never tell you to not leave me, but it scares me at the same time, ya know?"

"It's okay to be scared. But we're not leaving you. Well, Benji moved out so he can get railed every night, so lucky him, I guess." He smiled at me. "But we're the Wylde Street Boys. Like the musketeers, just hornier."

I chuckled. "I fucking love you, you know that?"

"Well, I do now because you told me." He grinned and nudged me with his knee. "We're not going anywhere."

I let out a long sigh. It was heavy, yes, but I did feel better. Underneath the surface ache, the deeper wound felt a bit more bearable.

"So," he said, his tone brighter. "Your two daddies . . . did they watch your solo video?"

I shook my head. "Not yet. I still haven't watched it through yet."

"We could watch it now. You and me," he said, far too eagerly. "I'll need a wank later so it's good timing."

I sighed. "I really shouldn't be surprised by anything that comes out of your mouth, and yet . . ."

"And yet, you love me. You said you did. You can't take it back." He clapped his hands, excited. "Let's watch. I just know it's gonna be good."

Gawd.

I was going to have to get used to this. This is what we'd agreed to do. It was our ticket out of this life. Normally I had no issue with sexual modesty, but this felt personal.

I'd chosen to wear my skirts and be true to myself, and maybe that was my subconscious trying to break free before my head and heart had caught on.

I needed to do this.

And he knew about my skirts and he accepted me fully. So even though this felt like I was flaying myself wide open, I trusted Fitch.

He loved me for who I was.

All of me.

So I grabbed the laptop and, sitting beside my best friend, I pressed Play.

And then I immediately hit Pause.

"If I say their names in this," I said. "You have to promise me—"

"Yeah, yeah," he said, waving his hand. "I already heard their names once and I'm just pretending for everyone's sake that I didn't."

Well . . . that was true.

Fuck.

I hit Play and we watched.

Me on the bed on my knees, nothing but my legs, the short frilly pink skirt and my naked tummy was visible.

"Well, it's hot as fuck already," Fitch said. "You're gonna be more popular than me, just so you know."

It wasn't long before the video-me was sinking down on the dildo, rising up on my knees only to sink a bit lower on the way back down. I was vocal, moaning and whimpering for my daddies.

Yes, plural.

Then video-me was stroking my dick through my panties, which I had no recollection of doing. I'd been so into it, convincing myself that I was with Leon and Marek. That it was Leon's cock inside me, that it was Marek's hands on me, their whispered words of pleasure . . .

Then video-me was stroking myself, taking the dildo faster and rocking back and forth. "Daddy, please. Please daddy."

Fitch made a weird sound, and when I looked at his face, his mouth was open, his eyes were transfixed on the screen. He raised a hand. "Shh. Don't interrupt."

I chuckled and went back to watching too.

I was looking more at the lighting, the angles, the sound quality, and it was much easier then. To look at it objectively, the way I'd watched Fitch's video. I wasn't watching it as porn, I was watching it as a . . . producer?

I wasn't sure.

Then video-me was coming, the dildo firmly seated in my trembling arse, my cock shooting stripes of come, and my strangled cry and heavy breaths that followed.

I hit Stop and turned to Fitch.

He was still staring at the screen. "Fuck, dude." His wide eyes met mine. "That was so hot. It's definitely going into my wank fodder folder. Jesus fucking Christ." He let out a rush of air. "Thank god I'm seeing Dom tonight."

"So you were totally paying attention to things like lighting and sound quality, right?"

"Oh, sure," he said, making a face. "One hundred percent."

He absolutely was not.

"I didn't say their names, so that's good."

Fitch still seemed stunned. "You know what? I'm gonna go make another video. No point in wasting a hard-on." He clapped my shoulder. "Thanks, bro."

He stood up, and yes, he was sporting a bulge. "Okay, that's not weird, at all."

He laughed as he disappeared into Benji's old room, then he turned and poked his head out, smiling, of course. "This won't take long." Then he was gone.

I laughed and let out a long sigh. It had been a strange twenty-four hours, but I felt good. Happy, and even a little content.

I felt good about myself, and that was a first in a very long time.

While I was in an honest mood, I took out my phone and sent Benji a text.

How are things?

I miss your face

His text bubble appeared, then disappeared, and then my phone rang. It was him.

"Hey," I answered. "Everything okay?"

"Very. Just figured it was easier to talk than text."

"Okay, boomer."

"Fuck you."

He laughed. "How are things with you. I miss your face too."

"Good. I'm good. I just wanted . . ."

"You just wanted what? Are you okay?"

I laughed because it was kinda funny that they both assumed something was wrong with me when I decided to open up to them. "I think I had a bit of a breakthrough yesterday, that's all. I just wanted to tell you and Fitch that I really appreciate you both."

He was quiet for a moment. "Ky, are you sure you're okay?"

"I'm fine," I said with a laugh.

"I can come over today," he said. "Is Fitch there?"

"He is. He's in doing another video. He watched my video and apparently couldn't wait to see Dom tonight."

Benji laughed. "Then I should absolutely come over and watch it."

I snorted because he was just as weird and perverted as Fitch. And while it was on the tip of my tongue to tell him not to worry, not to come over because I didn't want to be a bother, I stopped myself. Because spending the day with the two of them sounded perfect. "Okay, see you soon."

WHEN BENJI ARRIVED, I was in my room. "Okay," Fitch said loudly. "He's here. Come out and show us."

I took a deep breath and slow exhale, then opened the door and walked out.

Wearing my lilac bubble skirt and dark purple mesh shirt.

Fitch was murmuring something to Benji, but he gasped when he saw me, his hands to his cheeks. "Beautiful. Do a twirl."

"I'm not doing a fucking twirl," I grumbled.

Benji was clearly surprised but caught on quickly. Whatever Fitch had mumbled to him had given him some warning at least. "You need some leg warmers and some bangles."

Fitch shoved him. "He does not." Then he looked at me. "I mean, it would look good."

I rolled my eyes, but my heart was full to bursting. "Is it okay?"

"You look great," Fitch said softly. "I'm proud of you."

Benji looked between us, smiling, clueless. He looked at Fitch's tiny boy shorts and crop top that had *Come Bunny* with a cute rabbit on it. "Did I miss something?"

Fitch snatched the purple nail polish off the coffee table. "Yes. Now sit down and watch our porn videos while we fill you in on everything while I practice painting nails, and you can show us your videos and tell us all about how perfect Nolan and his big dick is."

Benji didn't even blink. He just rolled with it. So I sat there, wearing a skirt in front of them for the first time, and Fitch did my nails—very badly, but he tried his hardest—and we watched more videos, talking, laughing all day.

Just the three of us.

It wasn't even like the old days. This was the new us. The new me. The real me.

And I was so freaking happy.

I was walking on cloud nine. The happiest I could ever remember being.

And as the afternoon rolled on, I was getting giddy with butterflies knowing I'd be with Leon and Marek again tonight.

I was so excited to tell them about my day. To let them see how happy I was. To thank them for being the reason.

My ride share picked me up on time. Sometimes Leon and Marek picked me up themselves; sometimes I caught a lift. It depended on their schedule. I knew they were busy, so when Marek texted me to give me the details, I thought nothing of it.

I got to their house and Marek greeted me with a warm smile that sent jolts of warmth through me. "Oh my darling, come in," he said, taking my hand. He noticed my nails and hummed approvingly. "Mm. Lovely."

"Fitch painted them," I said, as if that explained the bad job. "I have so much to tell you both. I had a wonderful day with Fitch and Benji. I wore a skirt around the flat for the first time," I blurted out. Then I looked around the very quiet house. "Where's daddy? Is he upstairs? I can wait to tell you both at the same time."

Marek's smile faltered a little. "He's not here tonight. It's just you and me."

I stopped cold.

"What?"

Marek took my hand and led me to the couch and my brain was short-circuiting.

This was bad.

This was very bad.

"Is he . . . ?"

"Darling, he's fine. He's just in Melbourne."

"Melbourne?" This didn't make sense. "What's he . . . ? Why aren't you with him? You're never not with him. Did something happen?"

Marek's eyes filled with kindness. "Oh, princess, no." He put his hand to my cheek. "You're such a sweet boy. Everything's fine. We're fine. This was an emergency legal matter that couldn't be helped. We were both going to go, and normally we would. But after last night, with how you were, we felt it would be best if I stayed behind. We didn't want you to feel abandoned."

"Abandoned," I mumbled. "With how I was? What does that mean?"

Marek took my hands and held them tight. "You were so upset, worried with things changing and feeling left behind, we couldn't cancel on you the very next day. What message would that send you?"

I opened my mouth to answer, to say something, but not sure where to start.

"I never meant to be a bother. I never meant to . . ."

"Oh, Kylan, darling," he said fondly. "You are no bother. No bother at all. Actually, you're the opposite of that."

I shook my head, confused. "But you're never apart. You're never not together. And now you are because of me."

He chuckled and shook his head. "Of course we have nights and days apart," he said. "Not very often, that's true. But it does happen."

I wasn't sure what to think. What to make of this.

"You stayed because of me?"

He sat back, crossed his legs, and smiled. Relaxed, comfortable, happy. "I did. Leon and I decided together that it was the right thing to do." Then he did a little nose scrunch that made his moustache twitch. It was cute. "Well, I was feeling anxious about it and Leon told me to stay. I didn't even have to say what I was feeling, he just knew. He felt the same."

Oh.

"I'm going to fill you in on a very poorly kept secret while he's not here," Marek went on to say. "He might appear outwardly stern and stoic, but he's a big old softie."

I smiled at that. "I know."

Marek chuckled. "And he has a soft spot for you, darling. About the size of his whole heart."

I stared at him, heart racing, feeling my cheeks flood with heat. "Oh."

"We both do. So please don't fret about him not being here tonight."

All I could do was nod.

What a day.

What a fucking day.

"You had a good day?" Marek prompted.

I nodded, getting teary again. "The best day." Then I shrugged. "But now . . ." I wasn't sure how to say this.

"But you wanted to tell Leon?"

Was that hurt in his eyes?

Oh, dear god.

I grabbed his hand. "Both of you. It's always both of you. It's not him more than you, please understand. I need you both equally. The same. Both. It's not against you. It's—"

He smiled, taking my hand gently. "I know, darling."

"Fitch asked me if I had a favourite," I added, no clue why. I just needed him to understand. "And I couldn't choose. Neither. It's both. You're a pair, a matching set, interlocking pieces. I need you both."

"It's okay, Kylan," he said, still kind, still calm. He

always looked at me with such fondness. "I miss him too. We can miss him together, hmm?"

I nodded, gripping his hand. "Okay."

"We could FaceTime him later if you like?"

"I would like that, very much," I said.

"And you and I can have a special night. I was thinking we could order pizza and ice cream. Just for you and me. And watch a movie or something fun. How does that sound?"

Umm. I made a face. "Uh . . ."

Marek laughed. "Oh, sweet boy, I know what you're thinking. We don't have to do anything sexual. Would you find it strange without your other daddy here?"

I tried to think . . . "I don't know. Maybe? I'm just very used to both of you. I'm not used to this. Would he be mad at us? Would he be missing out? I don't want to hurt his feelings either."

"Would you feel more comfortable talking about it with daddy when we FaceTime later?"

I nodded, relieved that he even thought to suggest such a thing. "Much."

He gently touched under my chin. "You're the best boy."

I snuggled into him. "Thank you, daddy. And thank you for thinking of me, for staying here to be with me. I'm a very lucky boy."

He cuddled me for a long moment, just rubbing my arm and back, and every so often, kissing the top of my head. It was everything safe and warm, though Leon's absence still clung to me. "Why don't you go up and get changed," Marek suggested. "Wear whatever you want, and I'll order the pizza and the ice cream. Do you have homework to do tonight?"

I sat up and met his warm gaze. "I do, yes, daddy."

"Bring your books down," he said firmly. "Our fun night can begin after your work is done."

He knew I needed this normalcy. This night was different enough, especially on the back of yesterday, and Marek understood that our usual routine would make me feel better. I leaned in and kissed him, smiling. "Thank you, daddy."

I ran upstairs and chose an outfit I knew Marek favoured. It was a small, pleated school skirt, grey-and-pink tartan that barely covered my small black panties.

I chose the matching pastel pink school vest, no shirt underneath, and dotted on some pink blush and lip gloss.

Marek always hummed when he saw me wear this outfit. And if I was doing schoolwork . . .

I picked up the black vibrating butt plug, unsure. He'd said there'd be no sex tonight, and I understood why. But that was another out-of-routine thing that made me uneasy.

As much as I wished Leon was here, I didn't want Marek to think he wasn't my daddy in his own right.

Because he was.

Before I could overthink it and spiral, I took some initiative and made the decision on my own.

I went back downstairs to find Marek on the sofa, legs crossed, reading the financial newspaper. He looked up at me and did a double-take, his smile faltering, and he made that delicious humming sound again.

"I'm dressed for school, daddy," I said softly. Then I handed him the small remote control.

He knew what it meant.

He looked at it, then at me, and waited for my explanation.

"I know tonight is different but you're still my daddy, even if Leon's not here. And there's no reason why things have to be so different just because one of my daddies isn't here."

His lips curved up into a smile, his moustache twitching.

But he didn't say anything and that made me nervous.

"Is that alright, daddy? You don't have to turn it on, and I know you said no sex without him, and I appreciate that. This isn't about sex. This is about you and me. A daddy and his boy. And it makes me feel normal to wear it and give you the control, because that's what I'd normally do, and I don't see why that should change . . ."

Marek set the newspaper aside and stood up. He was close enough that his body heat made me dizzy. Or maybe that's because I wasn't sure I'd breathed in the last two minutes.

He hummed again, low and rough, as he looked down at my outfit. "You wore this for me?"

I nodded. "Of course, daddy. I know you like it."

Then he put a hand to my neck, sliding it down over the vest, squeezing my pec before snaking his hand down my belly and around to my arse. He cupped me and pulled me against him, giving my arse cheek a good grope. "And this?" he murmured, pressing the remote on.

The vibrating butt plug buzzed to life, and I moaned as I fell into him, on my tippy toes, the vibrations lighting up fireworks first in my arse and my balls, then sparking throughout my whole body.

He held me close, his hand still on my arse, feeling the vibrations, no doubt.

And then the vibrations stopped.

The buzz was gone, leaving residual embers sparking in my bones. I sagged against him, gasping for breath.

"I'm proud of you, princess," he murmured, both arms now holding me tight. I buried my face into his neck, relishing his strength and warmth.

His words.

"You knew I needed something like this," he said. "Our routine. To be a daddy for you."

I looked up at him. "You are my daddy. Even when Leon's not here."

He brought me up for a kiss, soft and slow, a hint of tongue. "You're so perfect, darling."

I beamed at his compliment. "I just want to make you happy."

He laughed incredulously. "Oh, you do more than that, princess." He kissed me softly. "Now, get some schoolwork done."

"Yes, daddy."

I took my usual spot on the floor, lying on my tummy close to Marek's feet. I could read my books and kick my feet, but it also gave him a great view of my arse in this tiny skirt.

I swear some nights, I could feel Leon's eyes on me, on my arse, and I could feel his desire rising just by watching me.

Marek liked it too, of course. Glancing over every so often, his eyes raking over my legs and this outfit. I forgot about the no-sex thing for a minute and spread my legs, and he punished me by turning the butt plug on.

Not as strong as before but enough to make me gulp and groan, clenching hard and fisting the soft rug.

I wanted to cry out but bit it back, and when I drew my legs back together, the vibration subsided.

"Thank you, daddy," I whispered, breathless.

"Hmm," Marek hummed, and when I looked up at him, I could see he was holding his phone up. "Say hello to daddy?"

I looked at the screen, and there was Leon. His torso and smiling face, anyway.

"Oh, daddy," I said. "I miss you."

He grunted. "I miss you too, boy. Both of you. I'm sorry I couldn't be there tonight."

I sat up on my knees, resting on my haunches, wiggling a little because of the butt plug. I straightened out my skirt and smiled at the screen. "It's okay. I know you're very busy."

"You're doing schoolwork, I see?" he said.

I nodded. "Daddy's watching over me."

Marek smiled at me, keeping the screen on me for Leon. "Hm. He's being a very good boy. He's even wearing a plug." He held up the remote in front of the phone so Leon could see it on-screen. And then he pressed the button again, and I yelped out a moan, closing my eyes tight, trying to regain some composure. It wasn't easy when I was on my haunches like this; the jolt of it almost drew me up to my knees.

"Oh, daddy," I cried out.

"Fuck, boy," Leon murmured on-screen.

The vibration stopped and I sagged back to my haunches, heavy with the exertion. "I wanted daddy to know he's still my daddy, even if you're not here. But he won't fuck me while you're not here. I promise."

Leon smirked. "Hm. Why's that, boy?"

"Because it's not fair if you miss out, daddy," I replied. I looked at Marek for reassurance, and he smiled. "I have two daddies, equally."

Marek turned the phone around so Leon could see his face. "See? He's loyal to you."

"To both of you," I corrected.

Marek's eyes cut to mine, and he smiled. "I stand corrected. To both of us."

I leapt up and crawled up Marek to lay my head on his chest. "I need both my daddies the same."

Marek chuckled, his arm going around my shoulder. "I told you he was the very best," Marek said.

Leon smiled. "I know he is. But if you want to play with him, Marek, my love, I could watch. Then no one misses out."

Marek hummed out a moan, his hand going down to

my arse, giving the plug a jiggle. "He is wearing my favourite outfit."

Leon grinned. "I noticed."

"What do you think, boy?" Marek asked. I lifted my head so I could see his face. "Do you want to give daddy a show?"

I nodded, then looked at the phone screen. "If daddy says so."

Leon was already unthreading his belt and unbuttoning his pants. "Fuck yes," he said, his hand over his briefs, stroking his fat cock.

So I took the phone and set it on the coffee table, ensuring the best angle. I was getting good at that now. "Can you see me, daddy?"

"Yes, boy."

Marek was back then with some lube, and he knelt me on the sofa and pulled my panties down to expose the plug.

Then he turned it on.

I shot up, arching my back, and Marek caught me, wrapping his arm around my chest and keeping me pressed against him. The shocks of the vibrator were firing through my bones, my veins.

I was trembling, almost crying. "Daddy, please."

He switched it off and, not giving me a moment to recover, bent me over, slowly extracting the plug. "Look at this perfect gape," Marek said, no doubt showing Leon on camera. "So fucking hot."

"Fill him with your cock, baby," Leon said. "Plug him right back up."

With a drizzle of cool lube and the sound of Marek's zipper, he gave no warning, no preamble. Just gripped my hips and sunk his glorious cock into me.

All the fucking way.

Balls deep, in one push.

Yelping, I gripped the sofa, the cushions, trying to pull away from the intrusion. "Daddy, daddy," I cried.

"Take his cock, boy," Leon said. "I know you can take it. Just like that. Grip him harder, baby. Hold that arse on your cock. That's so fucking hot."

Marek let out a wild groan, impaling me with every fucking inch and no remorse. "This slutty boy," he hissed. "Teasing me with this skirt. He knows how much I like it. Wore it just to tempt me."

"Fuck him hard," Leon urged him. "Bury that load deep."

I cried out as he began to fuck me, arching my back as I clawed at the sofa. Marek's thrusts were hard and sharp and so fucking deep.

So fucking perfect.

"Can you see me fucking him?" Marek asked, voice tight.

"Yeah, baby. So turned on right now. You're gonna make me come."

I looked over my shoulder, seeing the screen. Leon was pumping his cock, getting off on watching us.

It filled me with pride, and god help me, it turned me on. "Oh daddy, fuck yes."

The need for release was too hard to ignore. I let go of

the sofa and began stroking my cock, and pleasure, sharp and blinding, shot through me.

I came hard, crying out, and Marek slammed into me, driving my orgasm higher. He roared as he came, his cock spilling his seed deep, deep inside me.

Every pulse, every spurt, every grunt and groan.

It was heaven.

The room spun and Marek's hold on me, my hips, my back, became tender circles, gentle touches. He was panting, and Leon was too. I looked at the camera, seeing his spent cock and stripes of come across his belly and chest.

"Thank you, daddy," I whispered. "Both of you."

Leon's face, smiling back at me, proud as hell. "That was so good. I should go away more often."

"No," I cried. "No, daddy."

Leon moaned contentedly. "Marek, my love, are you okay?"

Marek chuckled and slowly pulled out of me. "I'm so fucking good right now."

"Yes, you are," Leon purred.

Marek inspected my hole, showing Leon. "Look at this. Needs your load, baby."

"Soon."

Then, surprising us all, the doorbell rang.

I straightened up and Marek laughed as he fell back onto the sofa. "That'd be the pizza." He tapped my arse cheek. "Fix your skirt and go answer the door, princess. But take your panties off. I wanna see my come run down your leg when you do."

I pulled my panties down, giving Leon a pretty view,

and ran to the door, enjoying the feeling of no underwear, the skirt on my sensitive dick. "Coming," I called, and I heard Marek chuckle.

I took a second to pull my vest down, ensuring there was no come on it, and opened the door.

The pizza guy, about my age, tall and broad, smiled and was about to say something, then . . . stopped. "Well, damn," he mumbled. He seemed to forget he was holding the box with a bag on top, too busy looking at me.

I'd never let anyone I didn't know see me in a skirt, let alone in one that resembled an anime girl's school uniform.

Then I felt it . . .

Seepage. Marek's seed was oozing out of me.

"Everything okay?" Marek called out.

"Yes, daddy," I replied. "Is it paid for?"

"Of course, princess," Marek yelled.

The pizza guy's eyes widened. I grinned and took the box. "Have a good night."

"Not as good as yours, apparently," the pizza guy mumbled.

"I highly doubt it," I said with a laugh and closed the door. I skittered back to the lounge room. Marek was cleaning the sofa and Leon was gone. It made me sad. "Oh, did daddy have to go already? He didn't say goodbye."

"I told him we'd call him again at bedtime." Marek came and took the pizza. He slid it onto the table and took my face in his hands and kissed me softly. "He was very happy with you."

I looked up at him. "He was?"

Marek smiled. "As am I."

I squirmed, trying to clench my arse, not wanting to make a mess. "Daddy, I think I'm leaking a little. I want to keep your seed inside me."

Marek's nostrils flared. "Turn around," he ordered and faced me to the table and bent me over. "Let daddy take a look."

I bent over, knowing the skirt wasn't hiding anything.

Marek bent down, kneeling between my feet, his hands on my arse, and he massaged me. "Fuck," he whispered. "That's beautiful."

Then he stood up. "Stay there, just like that." He took his phone and snapped a few pics. "Daddy's gonna love this."

He palmed my arse cheek again, giving it a good wobble, making me leak some more. "God, I could fuck you again right now."

"Okay, daddy," I breathed, widening my legs, waiting . . .

Wanting more.

Marek laughed, a pained sound. "Stand up, princess. Go and get cleaned up. We'll have dinner. I'll put this ice cream in the freezer." He took the bag and headed toward the kitchen. "I'll set the table. Be quick, darling."

I raced upstairs and opted for the quickest shower ever. The detachable showerhead made for easy cleaning, and I opted for a cute cotton pink pyjama set and panties with cupcakes on them. I felt cute and adorable and ready for food and snuggles.

When I came back down, Marek had the table set for two, the pizza box open, and the television on. "Are you hungry, sweetheart?" he said.

I nodded. "I am."

"Do you feel okay?" he asked as I sat down.

"I feel great, daddy," I said. "I'm excited for ice cream and a movie and calling daddy again at bedtime."

Marek smiled as he sipped his glass of water. "Me too, darling. Me too."

I WALKED INTO OUR UNIT, slid my phone and key onto the kitchen counter, and slid dreamily onto the couch. Fitch was watching me, so I made a show of putting the back of my hand to my forehead and swooning.

He laughed. "Someone got thoroughly railed."

I chuckled. "Well, yeah," I allowed, "but it was more than that."

"Two daddies work you over extra well or . . . ?"

I held up one finger. "One. The other was in Melbourne."

Fitch stared at me and plonked himself beside me on the couch. "One. What do you mean? I thought you said—"

"Oh, the other watched via FaceTime."

Fitch's concern became a smile, then a grin. "Ah."

"And then we had pizza and ice cream, and we watched a movie in bed while—" I almost said his name.

"While the other daddy was on the phone with us. I slept so freaking well."

He nodded. "And?"

"And then I sucked his dick in the shower this morning. Sent daddy to work a very happy man."

Fitch clapped his hands and wiggled. "I love that for you."

I sighed. "And last night, I answered the door to get the pizza wearing a slutty schoolgirl uniform. First time I've ever done that."

Fitch clamped his hand on my arm and squeaked. "Oh my god, yes! And how was it?"

"He totally flirted with me."

"The pizza guy?"

I nodded. "Yep."

He waggled his eyebrows. "And? Did your daddy punish you for that?"

I snorted. "No. I had his come running down my leg, so I—"

The scream Fitch let out was eardrum piercing, and his hold on my arm was now bordering on too tight. He bounced up and down, making an odd stuttering sound. "Fuck yes, I want to be you when I grow up."

My laughter became a sigh. "I wish I could tell you everything. I probably shouldn't even say what I've said."

"I won't tell anyone," he said. "Well, okay. There's a good chance I'll be telling Benji about the come running down your leg while you're wearing a slutty schoolgirl uniform thing. Because that is hot as fuck, my friend. But it's not like you tell us their names or the ins and outs of what they do."

I gave him a smile. "Thanks. I know I've not been one to share shit with you or Benj, but now I've started, I want . . . It doesn't mean I don't trust you or that I don't want to tell you. I mean, yes, it's a contract. And I signed willingly. At first, I thought it was no big deal because I had nothing to lose. I mean, what could they ever sue me for? I have nothing. But now . . ." I shrugged. "I'd lose them and that would kill me."

Fitch slid his hand over mine. "You don't have to explain. I get it." He gave me a sad smile. "It's no longer about the money, right?"

My eyes met his and I shook my head slowly. "No."

"Your little perverted heart caught feelings. And I can't blame you. If I had two daddies who railed me twice a week, I'd become attached too."

"You do have a daddy that rails you twice a week."

He grinned. "Oh, and he does it so fucking well. My god." But then he held up two fingers. "But you got twice the dick, twice the attention, twice the hearts, twice the love."

I let out a slow breath. "It scares me," I admitted quietly. "Being attached to anyone, being vulnerable and putting myself in a position where I risk being hurt again."

He squeezed my hand. "I get it."

And he did. Totally one hundred percent understood.

His big eyes met mine and I could see the vulnerability there too. "But it's worth it, right?"

I sighed. "I don't know. I mean, I see what they have. I see how they love each other so completely. They are so attuned, so *in tune* with each other, they are just . . . so in love. They've been together forever and are more in love now than they were back then. That's rare, and I . . ."

Fitch squeezed my hand. "And you, what?"

"I don't know where I fit in," I replied. "I mean, I know where I fit in. And that's the problem. Because I don't. I don't fit in. Not permanently. Not like them. They're . . . a set. A matching pair, inseparable. And I'm . . . a fun little toy thing they play with a few times a week. I have no right to be mixing my feelings with . . . with what they have."

Fitch took a moment, his hand still firmly clasping mine. "Look, I don't know them. I don't know anything about them, really. But I can tell you what I do know. They're clearly into you. They're obviously happy with what you provide. And not just provided services. I know what you're thinking," he said, giving my hand a squeeze. "You say they're perfect, but if they were so utterly perfect, they wouldn't be looking for a third person."

I frowned at him. "Two people in a relationship isn't the default, Fitch. It's just what society tells us, what religion tells us is *normal*. There's no reason why three or even four or five people can't make it work."

He smiled. "I know that. But listen, if they were such a perfect match, if they completed each other so thoroughly, they wouldn't be looking elsewhere, right? So maybe something is missing from their relationship, and that something is you."

I stared at him. "What?"

"You. Maybe you're what's missing. On one hand you called them a complete and perfect pair, then on the other hand said that three people can fall in love. So which is it? Is two people *complete* or can it be more?"

"It's too early in the morning for you to be using my own words against me."

He smiled. "Don't tell yourself you can't be a part of their perfect relationship. Because maybe it's you who just made it perfect. Their missing piece."

I rolled my eyes and let out an almighty sigh. "You shouldn't fill my head with things like romance and hope. It's a dangerous thing."

He smiled happily. "It's a dangerous and wonderful thing."

"You're so head over heels, it's gross," I said, only half joking.

He didn't deny it. "So, you got any photos of the slutty schoolgirl uniform? I need help visualising it."

"No you don't. You're visualising it right now."

Fitch laughed. "Hell yes, I am. But all photos or pictures of a likeness would help."

I snorted out a laugh. Then I remembered . . . "There might be a pic from the site he got it from."

He gasped. "Please. Pleeeeease. I need to see it."

I went and grabbed my phone, searching for a likeness. There was actually a photo—the photo that Marek had sent Leon of me bent over the table with my comey hole on display—but I wasn't showing Fitch that.

I found a likeness image online and showed it to him. He gasped, taking my phone. "Oh, it's better than I imagined. Do you wear the cat ears too?"

I chuckled. "No."

He sighed dreamily. "I wish I could see you in it. Can you wear it around here one day?"

"It stays at their place. Sorry." Taking in his pitiful sad panda face, I held my breath. Because he'd watched my solo video and he was, at heart, a fucking pervert. "Okay, one quick glance and that's it. I'll hold my phone, you only get to see for half a second. Don't blink, okay?"

He nodded eagerly.

I found the photo that Marek had sent to Leon. "It's in our group chat," I mumbled.

"We have a group chat?"

"No, not us. Mine and . . . my daddies."

"Oh my god, that's so sweet," he whispered. "You have a little family group chat. Kysie, that's the cutest thing ever!"

I chuckled, because it kinda was. Looking at the photo, I tapped on the photo to enlarge it. "Okay, are you ready?"

"Never been readier."

I turned my phone around. His eyes went to the screen for one second before I turned it back around. Fitch's wide eyes met mine. "Oh, I was not ready for that," he whispered. "Jesus fuck, Ky. That was . . . that was hot. And awesome. And . . . and I forgot to look at the skirt. Was there even a skirt? Because all I saw was you bent over a table and your wet boy pussy—"

"Okay, we're never calling it that again."

Fitch laughed but then he closed his eyes.

"What are you doing?"

"Burning that photograph into my memory. Straight to the spank bank."

I shoved him. "Perv."

"Uh, excuse me, after that photograph, I'm pretty sure you out-perv me on every level."

"Like you don't have similar photos on your phone," I said.

"I do not."

I nodded to his phone. "Prove it."

He laughed as he began scrolling his photos. "Okay, so maybe a pic or two." He stopped at one and smiled like the devil. "Like this?"

He showed me the screen. It was him, or a close up I assumed was him, wearing nothing but a crop top, face down on a bed, getting railed by a thick cock.

I couldn't see much of Dom, but it was obviously him who took the photo. Just his abs and where his cock disappeared into Fitch's arse. "Dom took it so I could see it from his view."

"Nice."

He scrolled back a photo or two. "And here's one of me on my knees," he said, about to show me the screen when his phone rang.

Benji's name came up on-screen, so Fitch hit Answer and put the call on speaker.

"Hey Benj," Fitch said. "You're on speaker. Ky and I are just sharing our own porn pics. Wanna see?"

There was a beat of silence. No laugh or witty comeback. "Maybe later," he said quietly. "Uh, Nolan just called me. We have a date for my dad's first appearance with the new charges."

First appearance.

New charges.

Additional charges brought about by Benji's evidence, his statements, his testimony.

"Fuck," Fitch replied. "When? When is it?"

"A week from Monday."

"Do you need us to come over?" Fitch asked. He looked at me, and I nodded.

"Yes please," Benji whispered. "Nolan's on his way, but he can't stay long."

"We're on our way."

I stood up, pocketed my phone and grabbed my key, just as Fitch's phone rang again. It was Dom this time. "Hey . . . yeah, we just heard. Benji called. We're going around to see him now . . . Okay . . . Yeah, of course . . . Okay. Talk soon."

He ended the call and pulled on his shoes. "Everything okay?" I asked. "With Dom?"

"Oh, sure," Fitch said. "He was just ringing to tell me about the court date. He works with Nolan, so . . . I told him we were going around now, and he said good. And to call him straight away if we need anything."

I smiled at him, though it felt a little flat. "He spoils you."

Fitch came over to me and clapped my arm. "You get spoiled too, no?"

I sighed, unsure as to why my mood felt determined to spiral. "Yeah. I do, when I'm with them, sure. But . . ."

"But what?"

I shook my head and waved him off. "Nah, forget about it. I'm fine. Everything's great. It actually hasn't been this good, probably ever. I don't know why I keep wanting to sabotage my own happiness."

Fitch studied me for a second, surely about to say something, but in the end, he decided not to. "Come on, self-saboteur. We can talk about it later. When you've had some time to think about why you feel you don't deserve to be happy."

I rolled my eyes. "Thanks. Past trauma and over-thinking. What could possibly go wrong?"

Fitch laughed and held the door for me. "There ya go. Masking deep emotional wounds with sarcasm and humour. Who even needs therapy?"

I snorted as I walked past him. "You do. Benji, most likely. I'll continue to use porn and self-degradation like a normal person."

Fitch's laughter rang loud up the stairwell. When we hit Wylde Street, the sun did its best to improve my mood, though even that fell short.

I knew what was bothering me. Well, one of the things that was bothering me.

Despite how my life was actually looking up, I wanted more.

I had the security of the contract between me, Leon,

and Marek. And I did find comfort in that. But I wanted more. More of them, more than they could give me.

I had a taste of what love could feel like. As stupid as it was, as stupid as the fairy tale of love was—unrealistic, naïve, and ridiculous—I still wanted more.

I wanted to be included. I wanted Marek and Leon to want me more than just to be their little plaything. I wanted them to include me in their daily lives and not just when it was contractually convenient.

I wanted them to love me like they loved each other.

Like I loved them.

And I did love them, even though I refused to acknowledge that seriously, and fuck, I'd never admit it out loud to anyone.

But I was so in love with them. I loved the peace they gave me. I loved the security and the safety they afforded me. I loved how they encouraged me to learn, to make a better life for myself. I loved how they wanted me to grow.

I loved how they let me be myself.

They understood my need to be a femboy. They embraced my desire to be pretty and wanted, and that's exactly how I felt when I was with them.

Pretty.

Wanted.

And maybe that was why I loved them.

But I also wanted them to call me, like Dom called Fitch just to check on him and tell him to please call if he needed anything.

They weren't bound by a contract.

And I'd thought Fitch was at a disadvantage by that. But now I had to wonder . . .

Maybe it was me who was.

Get out of your own head, Kylan.

You're going to ruin a perfectly good thing by wishing you deserved more.

"Hey," Fitch said, giving me a shove. "Ky. Hop in."

I didn't even know there was a car waiting. He must have organised a rideshare. Or maybe Dom did it for him.

Marek and Leon do that for you too, Ky.

I know.

Stop overthinking shit.

"You okay?" Fitch asked once we were on our way.

"Yeah," I replied. "Gotta get out of my own fucking head."

"You know what it is?" Fitch said. "You're coming down from the highest orgasm high. It's a fucking hard crash, I swear."

I ignored the way the driver's eyes caught mine in the rear-vision mirror. "Maybe."

"The key, obviously, is to never stop fucking. Then you can't crash. Simple as that. It's like that saying to avoid a hangover, you gotta stay drunk. Same thing, just with a lot more jizz."

I laughed. "I'll keep that in mind."

All jokes aside, he slid his hand over mine. "You'll be okay," he whispered.

And that was why I loved Fitch.

The boy with the golden heart, pervy mind, and the filthy mouth.

We arrived at Nolan's place and it was a good distraction for me. Benji needed us, and it felt good to be concerned about him rather than myself.

Nolan was there, briefly. Clearly concerned, he knelt before Benji, took his face in his hands, and kissed him. Whereas Fitch puckered up beside him, I almost had to look away.

To be loved like that . . .

"Where's mine," Fitch had whined, pointing to his lips.

Nolan had smiled fondly, thanking the cavalry for turning up, and told Benji he'd be home as soon as he could.

Home.

God fucking dammit.

This funk was going to drag me under . . .

I didn't recognise myself. This me who needed reassurance, who needed validation, and support.

I'd been a lone wolf since I was a kid.

Maybe I needed the opposite of this. Maybe I needed to take a step back for the sake of self-preservation.

Maybe I was better off alone . . .

"Kylan," Fitch snapped. "Get your pretty arse over here." He was sitting on the couch with his arms around Benji. "This is a musketeer hug; your presence is required."

I joined them, reluctantly, but the second I was in that hug, the darkness got a little brighter. The tight band around my heart loosened its barbs just a fraction.

And I didn't feel so helpless.

I hugged them both and let myself breathe.

I tried not to think about Leon and Marek.

I tried to simply enjoy this moment with my two best friends, and I did my best to keep the darkness at bay.

Being with them didn't just help.

They'd saved me.

They'd saved me the same way Leon and Marek had, just in different ways. Cuddling with Benji on the sun lounger on the patio, Fitch making us laugh with his movie commentary, and of course, more discussions on our solo videos.

Benji had made some at Nolan's house, and Fitch was making them every chance he got. I was already falling behind on my quota, and we hadn't even uploaded anything yet.

"Well, at least I know what I'll be doing tonight," I said. "Making porn videos."

"Look at it like you're giving back," Fitch allowed. "For all that porn has given us."

Benji gave me a sympathetic smile. "No daddies tonight?"

I shook my head. "Tomorrow."

"You miss them," he said gently.

Oh boy.

"Yes, he does," Fitch answered for me. "He needs to tell them how he's feeling, and he needs them to rail him every day. I've seen a photo of what one daddy did to his pretty boy hole. Can't wait to see what it looks like after both."

"Jesus Christ."

Benji looked at me. "There's a photo?"

I sighed. "One I should not have even showed him because he was not supposed to say anything."

Fitch came over and weaselled his way onto my lap. "Awww, Kysie. Benji doesn't count. We're the musketeers, remember? One for all and all for one. That includes photos of your arsehole dripping with your daddy's goods."

"You know, an NDA doesn't have a musketeer clause," I said flatly. "I shouldn't have told you anything. Not a single thing. Now give me your phone."

Fitch happily handed his phone to me. "Are you airdropping the photo? Please say yes."

"No, I'm texting Dom to come get you."

He laughed and kicked his feet. "Yes, please. I'm gonna tell him to take some pics of what damage he does to my little boy puss—"

I picked him up off my lap and dumped him onto the couch beside us, and Benji laughed and laughed.

It felt good to see him smile.

It felt good to make him happy.

I got home later, walking into our dark and empty unit. Nolan had arrived home in a rush, collecting Benji in a hug. Dom had picked me and Fitch up, dropping me back on Oxford on their way back to Dom's place, but not before Fitch had almost climbed the centre console to plant a big old kiss on Dom's mouth.

"Are you being a brat?" he'd asked, smiling.

"Yes," I'd replied on his behalf.

Fitch had laughed, completely at ease, completely adored.

And I went home alone.

I used to love alone time. I used to love having the unit to myself, relishing in the quiet.

Now I turned on the TV for company, for background noise.

When I wasn't working, I used to go hang out on Oxford for the vibes, for the fun of it.

Now I didn't want to see any of it.

I could go down and work. I could find some random guy to take my mind off things and earn a few quick bucks.

I didn't want to do that either.

I didn't want anyone else to touch me.

I considered messaging Leon and Marek, and so help me god, I almost did. A dozen times.

But they didn't message me, so . . .

That told me all I needed to know.

I made a solo video. No dildo this time. Just a vibrating cock ring and some lube and a wank that made me feel worse.

I didn't bother with dinner. I had no appetite. I considered going downstairs and hitting up a bar. Not for a john or a quick fuck. I knew a dozen guys who'd suck my dick for free.

But maybe a drink or a hit of something else to make me feel better.

Drink and drugs weren't my thing. I'd promised Benji

and Fitch that I wouldn't touch it. We'd promised each other, sworn to each other that we'd never.

And that was the only thing that stopped me.

I didn't want to fall into that shit.

I just wanted to feel better. I wanted to forget everything for a while.

I stayed on the couch, watching shit on TV I didn't give a fuck about, drowning out the noise. I woke up in the same spot when the sun came through the window.

Fuck.

I certainly felt no better, but I'd made it through the night. And I'd be with Leon and Marek today and they'd help me forget . . .

They'd take me to that place in my mind where none of the bullshit weighed me down.

I got my usual text from them just before eight. It was the rideshare collection point confirmation for 10 a.m.

Thank fuck.

I just had to hold it together until then.

Just two hours and I'd be in my happy place. I would beg them both to fuck me for hours. I wanted them to hold me, to adore me, to use me.

Fuck, I needed it.

Except when I got there, I was strung so tight I could barely breathe. I walked inside, and the second I saw them both—not just one, but both—I burst into tears.

SIX
MAREK

SEEING KYLAN CRY, seeing his whole body sag, his face crumple, broke my heart.

He sucked back a heaving sob, and putting his hand up, he took a small step backward, then another, before he turned to run.

I had no clue what had happened. I'd been so excited for him to visit. Leon was especially looking forward to seeing him; he'd missed his last visit.

He missed him any day we didn't see him.

As did I.

But he took one look at Leon and his reaction was immediate. It was alarming and concerning.

And heartbreaking.

I'd never seen Leon run so fast. He got to the door the same time as Kylan did. Kylan pulled it open, and Leon reached over Kylan's head and pushed it shut.

Kylan spun around, afraid. Recoiling in actual fear.

He shrank back and Leon collected him in a crushing hug.

While I still stood by the dining table, unable to move, watching in absolute horror.

What the fuck had happened?

What did I miss?

Kylan sobbed and Leon held him. "Shh, baby," Leon soothed. "I got you. I got you, baby. You're okay."

Kylan cried harder, and Leon scooped him up like a child and carried him to the sofa. He sat with Ky in his lap, cradling him tight and letting him cry. Leon's gaze caught mine and he was as concerned and as clueless as I was.

I sat beside them, my hand on Ky's shoulder. "Sweetheart, you're okay. We're here, darling. You're safe here."

And that just made him cry even harder.

This boy, this poor sweet, sweet boy.

Leon kissed his head. "Your daddies are here."

He fisted Leon's shirt and we waited for him to cry himself out. I stroked his hair and he closed his eyes. He looked exhausted, and I wondered if he'd fallen asleep in Leon's arms.

Leon's eyes asked me all the questions.

What the hell happened?

What's wrong?

Did someone hurt him?

Did we do something wrong?

All I could do was shake my head.

I don't know.

"I'm sorry," Kylan mumbled. "I don't know why I'm like this."

Leon squeezed him and I rubbed his back. "It's okay, darling," I whispered. "Don't be sorry."

"You scared me," Leon said. It probably wasn't the best thing to say in that moment, but it was the truth.

He'd scared both of us.

Kylan sat up, alarmed and crying again. "I'm sorry."

"Don't be sorry, boy," Leon replied, softly wiping Ky's cheek. "But you need to tell us what's wrong. We can't help you if you don't tell us. Did something happen?"

He shook his head and shrugged. "No . . . Yes. I don't know."

"Did someone hurt you?"

"No," he said. "I can't be with anyone else. I don't work. I can't . . . I won't have anyone else touch me but you two." He cried again. "I belong to you both, even if you don't belong to me."

Wait . . .

What?

"Kylan," I began.

"I don't know how to do this," he cried. "I thought I could. I thought I could keep it all separate, but now I don't know."

The more he said, the more confused I became.

"You don't know how to do what?" Leon asked. "Be with us?"

"Yes!" he cried. "I want more. I mean it's more than I've ever had. It's more than I ever dreamed I would ever have." He sobbed, fresh tears rolling down his face. "But it's somehow not enough. I came here with nothing. I have nothing. No one. I'm so fucking alone it kills me, and then I get a taste of this, of what I could have, but it . . ." He screwed his face up. "I don't even know. It feels just out of reach. What I want is so close I could even hold it, but it's not mine. It will never be mine and it fucking kills me. This is killing me. Because I never wanted anything before." He was mad now. "I never needed anything or anyone, and I was doing just fine without it. I could be numb to it all and nothing would hurt me. And now . . ."

He looked at me, then at Leon, his eyes wide and so terribly sad. "And now it hurts so fucking bad."

I wasn't sure what to say.

I had no words. I was still trying to get my head around everything he'd just said, and I wasn't sure I was following.

The bottom line was clear though.

"We failed you," I whispered. Both Leon and Kylan's eyes flashed to mine. I rubbed Ky's back. "You're confused and hurting and that means we didn't do our jobs."

The pain in Leon's eyes hurt more than anything I'd experienced in my life. Then he looked at Ky. "Are you . . . are you saying you don't want this? Do you want out of the contract?"

"I don't want the stupid fucking contract," he said, and he climbed off Leon's lap and scampered to the end of the sofa like a scared baby animal. "I want you to want me without a contractual obligation. I thought I had security in that stupid NDA. I thought it meant something. I thought it was a security blanket. But it feels like it's suffocating me."

"Then we'll get rid of it," Leon said.

Ky gasped, his eyes wide with fear. Panicked, he reached out and grabbed Leon's arm. "No. Please don't leave me. I don't want you to leave me. I don't know what I'd do without you . . ."

And I think I finally understood.

The pieces of this messed-up jigsaw puzzle were finally taking shape.

He didn't want the contract. He wanted more. He was numb to everything before and now he wasn't, because now he was *feeling*.

He was in love with us.

"Ky, sweetheart," I whispered.

"I don't want your pity," he said. "And I don't want the NDA but please don't get rid of me. I will take anything you give me. I thought I could leave but I can't. I thought being with you knowing you'd never love me would kill me," he shook his head, more tears spilling down his cheeks. "But not being with you at all would hurt so much worse. I'm pathetic and greedy, and I shouldn't want more than you already give. You already give me so much. But I want more. I want this. I want you both, and I know I can't have it . . . I saw Fitch with Dom, and Benji and Nolan, and they're so in love and I thought . . . I want that. Why can't I have that? Because you two have each other, and I'm not part of that, that's why. You know I once told Fitch the whole daddy thing wasn't real, just a fantasy you played until you went back to a reality where we don't exist. And now look at me. I fucking fell for it. God, I should have never let myself feel anything. I'm such an idiot." He shook his head again, wiping his nose on the back of his arm. He stood up. "I should go. I'm really sorry. I'm so sorry. I'm so fucked up. I shouldn't have come here today. I wasn't gonna and I should have known better."

"Ky, wait," I said, getting to my feet as he took a step back.

He shook his head. "I can't stay. I'm sorry."

He looked at Leon, and I looked at Leon. And Leon just sat there, dumbstruck and so fucking sad.

What did that mean?

Was he just letting him go?

Was this over?

"Leon," I tried, fighting my own tears. "Say something."

He looked at me, defeated, and shook his head.

Kylan sobbed, turned, and ran.

And we did nothing to stop him.

He was just gone. The front door slamming behind him a loud and heartbreaking goodbye.

"Leon," I whispered, tears spilling down my cheek. "What the fucking hell?"

He closed his eyes slowly, his face a mask of sadness. "Marek, I think we need to talk."

I WASN'T ready for that.

I wasn't prepared for Leon's words. To think, for one moment, since the day I'd met him that I might ever doubt our love.

I felt cold and clammy, wooden and heavy.

"What?" I managed, merely a breath. "What do you mean?"

"We need to talk," he said again, tone flat.

Defeated.

"About us," he went on. "About this. About him. About . . . us."

He looked up at me then and tears welled in his eyes.

My insides felt wrong.

Twisted and strung too tight, hot and burning, cold as ice.

"Leon?"

He held out his hand for me, and I took it. I always would. It was habit, instinct.

"What are you about to tell me?" I murmured. "Because that"—I gestured to where Kylan had stood—"was terrible and awful, and my heart is breaking, but Leon, you're scaring me."

I didn't realise how much I was trembling until he took my hand.

"I love you," he said. "I always have. I always will. From the moment I laid eyes upon you. The day you said yes to marrying me was the happiest day of my life, second only to the day you said, 'I do.'"

I couldn't stop the tears. "I love you too."

"But . . ."

"But what?"

"But this isn't working."

I sobbed and pulled my hand free. "What?"

He snatched my hand back. "Not us, Marek. I mean with him. It was different with him from day one and we both knew it. He was . . ." Leon's chin wobbled and he sniffled. "I think we should let him go."

I shook my head.

Because I didn't want that, and I was sure Leon didn't either.

"But he was—"

"He was too close," Leon said. "Too perfect, too much. And you said it yourself. We failed him." A tear rolled down his cheek. "We weren't ready for someone like him. When we agreed to seeing him regularly, we said we'd discuss things open and honestly. And we agreed that if either one of us wanted out, we'd end it. We'd put us first, always."

That was true.

As much as it hurt.

And it did fucking hurt.

"I won't risk losing you," Leon whispered. "You are the love of my life, Marek. I never thought for one second I'd . . ."

He shook his head and sighed.

"And you never thought for one second you'd what?" I said, unable to take the bite out of my tone. "Fall in love with another man? Fall in love with Kylan?"

Leon's eyes cut to mine, and I knew it was the truth.

I sobbed, my hand to my heart. "I love him too."

He took my face in his hands and kissed me softly. "And that's why we need to let him go. We can't risk us. What we have is too precious. We'll just go back to us. Just us two. No third, no femboy, no games, no roleplaying, none of it. Just us. We'll be okay. And he will be too. He'll be okay."

We held each other and we both cried.

"He'll be okay," Leon whispered again, and I wasn't sure which of us he was trying to convince.

I FELT NUMB. For the rest of the day, I couldn't bring myself to talk to Leon. I didn't want to even look at him.

And perhaps that caused more pain than the whole Kylan situation. Because Leon and I had always been rock solid. We'd always agreed about every single thing. We were in tune, in sync, always. For over twenty years, he'd been my other half.

But I didn't agree with him on this.

Well, I knew what he was saying was true. But I didn't agree with how it ended. I didn't agree with it ending at all.

Yet Leon seemed to make the decision for us.

And I was hurting. I was hurting because Kylan was hurting. That poor sweet boy.

Our boy.

And, for the first time in our relationship, there was a distance between me and Leon, and I wasn't sure I wanted to close it. I wanted to hold my line and let myself wallow in this pain and grief.

I was heartbroken.

And maybe with some time I'd see Leon's reasoning. Because if having a third person in our relationship could harm what Leon and I had, then part of my rational brain knew that what Leon had said was correct.

He was right about that.

We should protect us first, at all costs. That was always our rule.

But we were different now.

The *us* part of the equation had changed.

Kylan had changed us.

And I wasn't sure I wanted to go back to who we were without him.

"Are you okay?" Leon asked.

I looked up at him from the chaise. I called this room the music room because of the grand piano, though it never got played. The dark blue walls, dark purple furnishings, large gold framed artworks, and lavish black-and-gold accents made for a space I found peaceful.

And a little melancholy.

Which was perhaps why I found myself curled up on the chaise, staring out the window.

"No," I replied quietly. "I'm not okay."

Leon's face fell. The pain and anguish on his face should have tortured me, but I almost felt glad that he was hurting too.

"Can I get you anything?" he asked.

Telling him he could get me Kylan seemed pointless.

I went back to staring out the window. "No," I murmured.

He stood there for half a minute, silent and sorry, but I didn't look at him. I couldn't.

And then he turned and walked out.

I didn't eat dinner. Couldn't stomach the thought of food.

I curled up on the sofa in the dark and watched old black-and-white foreign films without the subtitles. No idea what language they were. None of it mattered.

I fell asleep there. For the first time in our relationship, in our marriage, I'd refused to share a bed with Leon.

I was hurting.

And all I could think about was Kylan.

What was he doing? Where was he? Was he okay?

Was he safe?

I wanted to text him, to call him. But what could I say?

That I was sorry?

It still didn't change anything.

Would it hurt him more if I reached out?

I wasn't sure.

I kept replaying in my mind what he'd said. That he wanted us, that he needed to be with us. That he hated how he'd let himself feel anything.

That he wanted what we had.

That he wanted us despite knowing we could never love him.

I should have stopped him right there. I should have

told him that we did love him . . . Well, that I loved him. I was sure Leon did too. But instead we'd let him think we didn't, and then we'd let him leave.

We'd given that boy a glimmer of hope, and we'd snuffed it out when he needed it most.

When he'd needed us the most.

We'd failed him.

What had Leon said? We weren't ready for him?

But we could have tried.

I woke up to the feeling of being watched, and when I rolled over, my neck pulled, my head ached, and I felt ill.

Leon was standing there, dressed and ready for work.

"Marek," he said gently.

I gripped my stomach. "I can't go to work today. I feel sick." I sat up, my whole body stiff and sore. My heart felt like lead in my chest. I groaned as I got to my feet, my stomach rolling. "I'm sorry."

Leon went to help me, but pulled his hand back as if he was afraid to touch me. Afraid I'd reject him.

I hate this.

I hate all of this.

I was crying before I even got in the shower. I was crying when I crawled into bed, and I cried myself to sleep.

Everything was wrong.

Our perfect life, our perfect everything was wrong.

I slept for hours, which was hardly surprising considering I'd barely slept a wink all night.

I tried to eat some crackers mid-afternoon, but it was

like trying to swallow cardboard. So I made some lemon tea, but it was no better.

I wanted to text Kylan a dozen times, but didn't know where to start. And in the end, I had to let him know I was sorry.

> I'm so sorry.
>
> I hope you're okay.
>
> I don't expect a reply but please know I am so very sorry.

I didn't expect a reply, but by god, it didn't stop me hoping for one.

I held my phone and waited. And waited, and when no reply was forthcoming, no text bubble, my text still unread, it made me cry all over again.

I wanted to go to him, and I wondered if I should. I wondered if it would hurt Leon if I did. Would it be a breach of his trust?

I couldn't decide between them who to hurt the most.

Kylan was already hurting, and I knew Leon was too. But Leon had said to let him go.

My darling husband, the absolute love of my life . . .

I was so angry at him. Betrayed, hurt, and so fucking heartsore.

I still didn't want to see him. I didn't know what to say.

Something felt irrevocably broken and I didn't know how to fix it.

If it was fixable at all.

By four o'clock I was back in bed, utterly miserable. This dark hole of heartbreak felt insurmountable. Neverending.

I woke up again to Leon feeling my forehead with the back of his hand.

"Hey," he whispered.

I pulled back, not wanting his touch, his comfort.

I knew it hurt him, his hand going back to his lap. The sadness on his face, in the low set of his shoulders. But I couldn't stop myself.

He swallowed hard, nodded but said nothing.

I rolled over and closed my eyes, and he sat there for a long moment. "We need to talk, Marek," he whispered.

I said nothing.

"I'll make you some tea," he said.

"No, thank you," I whispered.

"Are you unwell, or . . . ?"

I didn't answer that.

"Marek, please," he said. "I'm trying here. I'm sorry. I wish I knew how to fix this."

"You know how to fix this," I replied, my voice hoarse and detached.

And then there was silence. And after a long moment, he stood up and walked out.

I didn't know where he slept, but it wasn't in bed with me. Maybe the couch, maybe the spare room, maybe even Kylan's room down the hall.

I wasn't sure why that hurt to think about.

Fuck this all to hell.

I went downstairs around six in the morning. I needed to stomach some tea before deciding if I could face work. To be busy and distracted with work and clients and meetings and phone calls would do me good, if I could just ease the twisted knot in my belly and the heaviness in my heart.

I switched the kettle on and Leon shuffled into the kitchen behind me. He looked terrible.

Pale, exhausted, and so fucking sad.

And my heart broke all over again.

"Leon," I tried, my voice breaking.

His eyes met mine, teary and so profoundly sad. "I'm sorry," he said. He put his hand to his heart. "Did I break us? Is that what's happening here? You and I were . . . we were always . . ." His chin wobbled. "I thought I was doing the right thing for us. Because it's been you and me, always. Never a doubt. And then he came along . . ." He shook his head and ran his hand through his hair.

My god, he looked so wrecked.

"And then he came along," I repeated.

"And now you won't look at me," he said, a tear running down his cheek. "I ended things with him to save us, and I broke us anyway."

"We didn't need saving," I said. "He did. Kylan needs saving, not us. That poor boy. God knows what he's going through right now."

Leon groaned and pulled at his hair. "You don't think I know that? You don't think I care?"

"Then why?" I yelled at him. "Why did you let him leave?"

"Because I love him," Leon yelled back.

And out of all the things, all the many things I might have expected him to say, that was not one of them.

"I love him," he said again, quieter this time. "And it scares me to death. That's why."

I shook my head, confused and unsure. "What? Why?"

"Because you are my entire world," he said, tears streaming down his cheeks. "The love of my life. My one and only." He sighed. "And then he came along. And it wasn't just you anymore. I love him the same as I love you, and it terrifies me. He was too close. He's too . . . Fuck, I couldn't risk losing you, so what else was I supposed to do, Marek? Tell me. How can I love someone else that isn't you?"

I went to him, this beautiful, frustrating, too-proud man, and thumped him on the chest. "You love him *with* me. You were supposed to love him *with* me, Leon. We love him together as much as we love each other. God, we fucked this up so badly. He was crying out for help and we fucked it up. We ruined that poor boy and any hope he had of trusting us, loving us."

Leon scrubbed his face. "How could we do that? How could we be more than we already were? You want to make him a part of us? For real? How can a third person join a marriage?"

"He was already a part of us. He was already *in* our marriage, Leon. Nothing had to change, except to love him even more."

He still looked torn, unsure.

"I know you're worried about us," I whispered. "And I get that. Hell, I am too. But Leon, he changed us. Who we were before him is not who we are anymore, and I don't know if we can ever go back to that. I see you with him and I love you more than I ever did before. I would watch you be with him, tend to him, love him, and it made me love you so much more. And that shouldn't be possible, but it is."

Then I poked him in the chest.

"But you hurt me when you sent him away. And fuck knows how much you hurt him because he won't reply to my texts, and I'm so fucking mad at you. You need to fix this. You need to make this right, Leon. And pray to god that boy forgives us because I will be mad at you for-fuck-ing-ever if he doesn't."

And then my phone rang, startling us both.

Kylan's name flashed on the screen and I snatched it up. "Hello? Kylan, baby. Please tell me you're okay?"

There was a beat of silence.

"Uh, no. It's not Kylan. It's Fitch. Is this Leon or Marek? Which one am I speaking to?" he asked sharply. "I guess it doesn't fucking matter. I don't give a fuck which one of you this is. I need to know what you did to him. What the fuck did you do to him?"

My mind scrambled, panic starting to build. "What . . . what's wrong? What happened, please, is he—"

"Save your bullshit. Get your arses over here right now and fix whatever the fuck you did to him." There was a beat of silence. "Now."

SEVEN
KYLAN

I DON'T REMEMBER MUCH.

I remember walking home, no thoughts, just one foot after the other. I have no recollection if I saw anyone, spoke to anyone.

I remember walking into an empty flat, grateful Fitch wasn't home.

I wanted to yell and scream, and I wanted to let it all out. I wanted to scream until my throat was sore, I wanted to pummel something until I dropped to the floor.

But no.

I took it inward.

It was safer that way.

Put it all in a box, closed the lid, locked it tight, and shut everything down until I felt nothing.

Until there was nothing left to feel.

It was safer that way.

It's what got me through this fucking life. It's what got me through a lot of things.

It would get me through this.

Though it sure as fuck didn't feel like it.

No matter how much I tried to lock this pain down, it kept seeping its way to the surface.

Raw and jagged, both aching and sharp.

I always knew it would hurt.

But I had no idea it would be this bad.

I crawled into my bed, pulled the covers over my head, and let the darkness have me.

I DON'T KNOW how long I slept.

I don't know if I slept at all.

I don't remember Fitch coming in the first time, but there was a glass of water by my bed and some crackers.

I do remember him sitting on my bed, his hand stroking my hair.

I don't remember what he said. I don't remember speaking. I don't think I did.

I don't remember if it was dark outside the window or light or when or if it changed.

I couldn't get up. I could barely fucking breathe.

All I wanted to do was sleep.

It was all I was capable of doing.

But then Fitch was pulling my covers back and pulling my arm to sit me up. "Come on, Kysie. I need you to get up. Just sit up for me."

God, my body hurt.

He put the glass of water to my mouth and made me

drink. "Come on, just sip it. There you go," he whispered. "I made you some toast and butter. Take a bite."

I bit it, chewed it, struggled to swallow it, and he made me sip some more water.

"I'm worried about you," he said, giving my shoulder a squeeze.

"They don't want me," I whispered, barely able to speak.

Fitch deflated with a sigh. "Oh man."

"I'm just . . ."

Fucked up.

Broken.

Not good enough.

Never good enough.

Lost.

Hollowed out and irreparable.

Unlovable.

"So tired," I mumbled, lying back down.

Fitch rubbed my arm, and I couldn't bear the sadness on his face, so I closed my eyes.

Next time I woke up, it was dark.

I could hear Fitch's mumbled voice, talking to who, I had no idea. Dom or Benji. Maybe he was on the phone, or maybe they were in the living room.

I didn't care.

I couldn't sleep any more, but I was still too tired and heavy to move so I just stared at the wall. Trying not to think, trying to squash all the pain into its box, but it was too big, too great.

So I stopped trying.

It didn't matter anyway.

I tried to clear my mind instead. I tried not to think about them, to think about the sadness on Marek's face or the cool resignation on Leon's.

I wasn't sure which one hurt the most.

It just all hurt.

So I went back to that place in my head where it was quiet and numb, between sleep and awake, like some astral fucking plane where I didn't exist.

Then it was light out the window again and Fitch was sitting on my bed with his phone to his ear. Then other voices; Benji, I think. Everything seemed so far away.

Then strong arms picked me up, cradling me, his heartbeat thumped in my ear.

His scent so familiar and comforting.

He smelled like home.

I looked up at him and he cried as he kissed my forehead.

Leon.

Crying.

"Daddy's here," he said, not even trying to hide his tears. "We're both here."

Then gentle hands brushed my face, rubbed my back, and when I looked over, I saw Marek.

Beautiful Marek with his tear-stained face.

And I wept.

Marek moved closer, both of them holding me, surrounding me. And the three of us cried.

"Oh, my sweet boy," Marek murmured. "We're so

sorry. We're here now. We're going to make this right. The three of us, together."

It made me cry even harder.

Leon rocked us. His strong arms felt like a safe haven, but I didn't dare to hope . . .

I couldn't bear to have it taken away from me again.

I wouldn't survive it.

"I'm so sorry I hurt you," Leon murmured. "I hurt both of you when I should have protected you and cherished you. I thought I knew what was best and I was wrong. God, I was so fucking wrong."

I looked up at him. Did he mean that?

He put his hand to my cheek, his eyes dark and sorrowful. "Please forgive me, Kylan. And Marek, I need you both to forgive me. I'm so sorry. We can work this out. We can get through this, I promise. I'll do anything."

Marek put his hand to Leon's heart. "I know you're sorry, my darling."

I tried to get up and they helped me sit on the bed. Leon took one of my hands and Marek took the other. And I tried to get my thoughts in order.

I was so tired. So empty. My chest was aching, raw and rough. "I . . . I don't know what you're saying. I can't think straight. I want to believe you, but I don't know what's real. I think I broke something. In my head. I used to be able to block the bad stuff out, but I can't. I tried but I couldn't do it."

Marek sobbed, bringing my hand to his face, his neck. And Leon put his arm around me. "Oh, Kylan, sweet boy.

We're here, this is real. We want you in our lives, in our home. We need you."

"But you said—"

"I was wrong. I was so wrong. Marek was right; we're not us without you. You changed us, and that scared me so much. I thought letting you go was the right thing to do, but it almost broke us. I've never been so scared in my life."

Leon? Scared?

He seemed to read the questions in my eyes because he nodded. "Terrified. I fell in love with you, Kylan."

My heart thudded to a stop, squeezing painfully. I felt dizzy.

He fell in love with me?

Leon squeezed my hand. "And it scared me to think I was taking something away from Marek. But he taught me that's not how it works, because he loves you too. And that doesn't mean we love each other any less."

They both love me?

Wait . . .

"It means we love each other more," Marek said. Then he put his forehead on my shoulder. "You said you wanted more. You said you needed us more than you thought we could need you, but Kylan my darling, we need you too. So much."

"Please say you'll come back to us," Leon murmured. "We'll work everything out. Everything you need, anything you want. We'll make it work, whatever it takes."

I sobbed out a cry. "Am I dreaming? Did my mind really snap? I think I've lost my mind."

"No, no," Leon replied. "You're not dreaming. We're here. We mean everything we've said. We love you, Kylan. And I'm so sorry I hurt you."

I cried harder, my shoulders shaking. "Everyone I ever loved hurt me. I tried to lock it away; I tried to lessen the pain." I pulled my hand free from Marek so I could push against my temple and then my sternum. I ached all over, inside and out. "And you say you love me, but if love feels like this, I don't know if I can stand it. I can't bear this. My heart and my head, everything hurts. I don't feel . . . right." I felt like crying but I was all out of tears. "I don't feel so good."

Leon felt my forehead, my cheeks, my neck. "You're hot."

"Of course he is," Fitch said from the door. He came in and knelt before me. "Kysie? Everything okay?"

I tried to smile for him. "Did you call them?"

"I had to do something. I'm sorry if it breached whatever clause in your whatever contract. But you were scaring me." He put his hand to my face and stopped, concerned.

"He has a temperature," Leon said.

"I'm just tired," I tried.

"He hasn't eaten or drunk anything in two days," Fitch told them. Then he glared at each of them. "Why do you think I called you?"

"We're indebted to you," Marek said gently. "I can never thank you enough."

"The contract is over," Leon said. "There are no clauses to breach."

I shot him a look. "What?" Panic began to bubble in my chest, squeezing my lungs. "But I—"

Leon smiled, his hand clasping mine. "I thought we could try dating. The three of us. And we don't need an NDA if there's nothing to hide."

I stared at him. "Dating? Me? And both of you?"

Marek let out a sniffly laugh and he looked at Leon with such fondness, with such love.

Then he looked at me the same.

Oh.

My head was starting to spin. Tired, dizzy.

Fitch took my arm. "I think he needs to lie down."

That was a really good idea.

"I think we should take him to hospital," Marek said, concerned.

"No," I said on reflex.

"Let's get him back to our place," Leon said. "We can have a doctor make a private house call—"

"Or he could stay here," Fitch said. "You know, because he lives here."

"Fitch," I murmured.

He sighed and studied my face. "You wanna go with them?"

I nodded. Because I really did. We needed to talk, about everything. But really, I just wanted to be with them. I needed them. I wanted to sleep in their bed. I wanted them to hold me, to comfort me.

To tell me I'd be okay.

Fitch nodded in return. "Yeah, okay. I get it." Then he levelled a glare at Leon. "I'll allow it. One more chance."

Leon surprised me by smiling. "Thank you."

"Look after him," Fitch added. "Make sure he eats and drinks some electrolytes or something."

"We will," Marek said. He stood up and helped me to my feet. "Come on, darling. Let's get you home."

EIGHT

LEON

TO SAY I'd fucked up was a huge understatement.

To say I'd taken Marek for granted was also up there in the stupidest things I'd ever done.

I'd taken him, his love for me, and his complete understanding and trust, and shaken its foundations until it'd almost come crashing down around me.

I'd never doubted us. Not for one second. And I should have.

I should have treated him as if he was about to walk away, because he very nearly did.

All because I assumed to know what was best. I assumed to know how he felt. I assumed to think that we'd just go back to the old us the second Kylan was out of our lives.

Oh, how wrong I'd been.

The hole Kylan left in our lives, in our home, in our marriage, was devastating. There was no going back to how we were.

He'd changed us.

He'd changed me.

I fell in love with him. I'd put it down to infatuation. A fleeting crush. The way he made my heart sing, the way he looked at me, how he looked at Marek; I was infatuated with everything about him.

I kept telling myself that's all it was.

As I'd told myself that Marek was infatuated with him too, that he had a crush on him the way I did.

That Marek and I were in love, and what we had with Kylan was different to that.

It had to be, right?

I couldn't possibly love another man the same way I loved Marek. I would never do that to him. He was the absolute love of my life. The reason my heart beat, the reason I woke up in the morning.

He was everything to me.

How could someone else be that as well? How could someone be equal to Marek in my life?

I couldn't let that happen . . .

Or so I'd thought.

To see Marek shy away from me, to feel him pulling back, was the most frightening thing to ever happen to me.

The thought of losing him almost killed me.

Like losing Kylan . . .

How could I have known Marek would feel the exact same? How could I know that I would cause Marek the same pain as I'd caused Kylan.

That I'd caused myself.

I couldn't lose Kylan any more than I could lose Marek.

That was very fucking clear to me now.

When Fitch had called and told us Kylan wasn't well, everything changed.

Priorities.

Pride.

We'd raced over, welcomed by a seething Fitch. He had every right to be mad at us. I'd seen him on Wylde Street and I'd seen the photo Dominic had once shown us, so I knew who he was.

He was protective of Kylan, and I'd be forever grateful that he'd called us. And that he'd called us out on our behaviour. I added phoning Dominic to my long list of things to do.

But getting Kylan home was my priority. Getting him showered and fed, getting him seen to by a doctor, getting him whatever he needed was my priority.

Righting this wrong.

Marek and I got him showered and dressed into some comfortable clothes and tucked him into bed. He sipped some electrolytes and took some Panadol with some juice and ate half a sandwich, but he really needed to sleep.

So we sat on the side of his bed and tucked him in. I held his hand and Marek stroked his hair until he was sound asleep.

When we left Kylan to sleep, leaving the door to his room ajar, I pulled Marek into my arms as soon as we were in the hall, and we held each other so tight.

I would never take him—either of them—for granted again.

"I love you," I whispered.

He nodded against my neck, his arms tightening around my back. "I love you too. And I love him, Leon. I need to know he'll be okay."

I pulled back and took Marek's face in my hands. "I love him too. He'll be fine; we'll make sure of it. He has us, for as long as he wants us. We'll look after him."

Marek's eyes were deep with sorrow. "The things he said. That he doesn't feel right, that he doesn't deserve love, it scares me, Leon."

I nodded. "Me too."

What Kylan was saying about locking down his pain and fear so he didn't feel anything at all was just awful. A coping mechanism, for sure.

"It's a response to trauma," I whispered.

Marek's bottom lip trembled, his eyes glassy. "Two days he just lay there, unable to eat or sleep. We did that to him."

I kissed Marek's forehead and pulled him against me for another hug. "We will help him. We can get him the best help. Medical, psychological, whatever he needs."

"We can't make that decision for him," Marek replied. "He needs to be the one who decides that."

I knew my instinct was to sweep in, make executive decisions, and fix things to however I deemed necessary, but Marek was right. I needed to respect Kylan's decision and take his lead on this.

"We'll ask him what he wants to do," I said. "And if

we need to prove to him that he's worth it, no matter how long it takes, then that's what we'll do."

Marek gave me a sad smile. "We almost fumbled this so bad."

"I almost fumbled this," I mumbled.

"No, not just you. Me too. We didn't talk. We didn't communicate the way we normally do. We were both so scared of hurting each other that we froze. And we've never done that before. We've never been like that before."

"We've never been in love with someone else before," I offered. "We've never navigated anything like this before. I was so scared of hurting you."

He nodded, teary again. "Same. I was so mad at you, and that was new for me. And we didn't talk it out."

"Because you couldn't even look at me?" I said with a smile, trying to lighten the mood.

"True." The smile he managed was tinged with sadness. "Maybe if I'd screamed at you to pull your head out of your arse, we could have saved everyone a lot of heartache."

I snorted. "True. So if there's ever a next time where you need to scream at me to stop being a jerk, please don't hold back."

He chuckled and sniffled, wiping his eyes and nose. "And I didn't stick up for myself," he said. "I let you dictate, because that's what we've always done."

"What? No, baby . . ."

He shook his head. "You've always led this dance, and I've always been happy that way. I've never had a reason to question that. You've always put me first, so why *would* I ever question that. You make choices for us, what's best for us, with me at the forefront of every decision. What I want, what I need, what makes me happy. Everything you've done has been *for me*, so when you said we should let Kylan go, I didn't protest. I thought maybe you were right, because I was in love with him and I didn't want to hurt you with that."

I put my hand to his cheek and studied his eyes. "Everything I've ever done has been for you. And I'm usually good with judgement calls, financial decisions, whatever you want, I would make it happen just to see you smile." I sighed. "But I was so wrong about this. I was wrong to assume, I was wrong to not ask. I was wrong to think I couldn't love you both equally. I won't make that mistake again. I promise. I will do everything I can to make you both happy."

Marek's gaze softened and he pressed his forehead to my cheek. "We're both going to need to learn how to better communicate. I don't know how threesome's work."

I froze. "Well . . . you kinda do."

He'd always had a penchant for threesomes. Ever since college, from day one he'd let me know he liked playing with a third. It was how our searching out additional partners all kinda started . . .

He gave me a shove. "You know what I mean."

"I do."

He looked up at me. "We need to sit down with Kylan and put everything on the table. Expectations, needs, wants. Everything. And maybe even make it a weekly thing so we never have this miscommunication thing happen again."

I kissed his forehead. "Okay. Marek, darling, we also need to prepare for the possibility that he doesn't want to be in a relationship with us. We are married and he's so young. He might not even want to go back to the daddies/boy roleplay." I shrugged. "We're already assuming he does."

Marek's whole face fell. "What if he doesn't? If he doesn't want to be our boy, that's not a deal breaker for me. I just want him with us, in any capacity. Just him. But if he doesn't want us at all, then . . . ?"

I sighed. "I don't know. But we'll get through it. Our first priority is making sure he's okay."

Marek sighed, still sad. "I'll go check on him. See if his fever has come down or if we should call the doctor." He shrugged. "I might make him some veggie soup. How does that sound?"

"Sounds perfect. I'll go check in with the office, make some phone calls, and check our emails. I'll just be downstairs. Yell if you need me."

Marek slipped quietly into Kylan's room, and I watched from the door how he sat gently on the side of his bed and felt Kylan's forehead with the back of his hand. How he stroked his hair and fixed his blankets.

Seeing him tend to him, care for him, made my heart full.

Would Kylan want to be in a proper relationship with us? I didn't know, but god, I hoped so.

Maybe he'd want to maintain our old agreement with a few modifications. Maybe he didn't want us at all.

Though when I'd suggested dating, the look in his eyes gave me hope that he wanted that. And he'd wanted to come here with us. We could have looked after him at his place, but he told Fitch he wanted to come home with us.

That had to be a good sign, right?

I had to believe he wanted to be part of us.

Or that he'd be open to discussing the possibility.

And what Marek said was true. We wanted him with us in any capacity. Whether that included Kylan being our boy, only he could decide that.

It was all up to him.

I SPENT some time in our home office. We'd never taken time off without notice before, and while I dealt with a few emergency emails and phone calls, our PAs and office manager handled rescheduling everything and managing clients who were demanding our time.

I told them we wouldn't be in tomorrow either. I said it was a personal matter, that Marek and I were both fine, but we were dealing with a family problem.

And that's what this was.

Family.

Sometime later, Marek came in with a small bowl of soup. It was thick and creamy and full of every vegetable we had in the house. He put the spoon to my mouth to let me taste.

"I know soup's not really a summer thing, but he needs some proper nutrition. Soup requires minimal energy to eat, and it will fill his belly," Marek said.

"It's delicious. And just what he needs."

"His temperature seems to have come down but we'll keep an eye on him. Maybe once the paracetamol wears off it'll spike again. We'll see how he feels about us calling a doctor when he wakes up."

I closed my laptop and stood up. "I'm done here. I told the office we won't be in tomorrow either. Regardless of how he's feeling, a day here with just the three of us is a good idea."

"Great idea." Marek stopped. "Oh. What about the Hysop case? They were coming in—"

"Taken care of, my love. Rescheduled and I emailed them myself."

He smiled at me. "Thank you."

"Everything else can wait. Let's go see if Ky's awake and how he's feeling."

Just then, somewhere upstairs we heard a toilet flush.

Marek smiled at me. "I'll go dish up some soup."

I KNOCKED LIGHTLY on Ky's door as he was getting back into bed. He looked up at me, shy and pulling the blankets up to his waist.

"Up for a visitor?"

"Of course."

"How are you feeling?" I asked as I came in.

"Okay. Still tired, somehow." He put his hand to his stomach. "I don't know if I'm hungry or if I feel sick."

I noticed then that his glass of water was now half-full, and I was glad he'd managed to drink some.

"It could be a bit of both," I suggested, sitting on the edge of his bed. "And maybe a bit of anxiety and worry."

His big blue eyes met mine and he nodded, his hands fidgeting in his lap.

I slowly put the back of my hand to his forehead. "Your temperature has come down, which is good. Marek's made you some soup. He's bringing it up now."

This surprised him. "Soup?"

I nodded. "Veggie soup, to make you feel better."

He got a little teary. "Oh. That's so nice."

I slid my hand over his. "I meant what I said before, Ky. We love you. I'm sorry I made a mess of everything before. I never meant to hurt you. And don't worry, Marek ripped me a new one for that."

He gave me a shocked smile. "He did?"

"Oh yeah. And I deserved it. When you're feeling better and you've rested enough, we'll sit down and talk about everything. I just want you to know that you're safe here and you're welcome here, no matter what you decide to do."

"Decide? About what?"

"About whether you want to be with us." I frowned. "I shouldn't be discussing this without Marek—"

"Discussing what without me?" Marek asked as he

came in. He was holding a tray with soup and bread, more juice and fresh water.

I stood up so Marek could slide it onto the bed beside Ky.

"I was just telling Ky he's welcome to stay here for as long as he wants until he's feeling better, and that he wasn't under any pressure to make any decisions."

"Good," Marek said. Then he helped Ky sit up against the headboard and spoon-fed him some soup. "Is that okay?"

Ky nodded and smiled at him. "It's really good."

My heart felt so big it could burst. And, if I was being honest, a little tender that he hadn't readily agreed to being with us.

Even though I'd just promised him there was no pressure . . .

"I'll leave you two to talk," I said quietly.

Ky's eyes shot to mine. "No. Please stay." He patted the far side of the bed. "Please stay with us."

NINE
KYLAN

GOING BACK to Leon and Marek's place had been the right thing to do. We needed to clear the air. We needed to talk.

And I needed to feel safe while we did that.

And *safe* was with them.

When I'd had enough soup, Marek took the tray and set it down on the dresser. He turned and looked as uncertain as Leon had when he'd said he'd leave the room, so I scooted over toward Leon and patted the bed.

"Stay," I said.

He smiled as he took his spot, and I was in my happy place once more.

In between them.

The three of us sat on my bed, resting against the headboard, and they each held one of my hands.

"I don't know what to say or how to start," I said quietly. "I just want to sit like this for a little while if that's okay."

"Of course it is," Marek answered quickly.

"We have all the time you need," Leon added. "We took today and tomorrow off work."

"You did? What for?"

Leon chuckled and Marek lifted my hand to kiss my knuckles. "To look after you," Leon said.

"I feel much better," I said. "You don't need to take time off for me."

"We want to," Marek said. "We need to."

I looked at him then.

"We need to talk," he continued. "The three of us. About everything. If this is going to work between us, we need to talk about it."

"But first we need to make sure you're okay," Leon said. "You weren't well this morning. Sick enough for your friend to be concerned."

"He called you," I said. At least, I was pretty sure he had.

Marek nodded. "Yes, thank god. He was really worried. We both were too."

I sighed. "I was just . . . It was just dehydration, I'm sure. I feel better now."

"It was more than that," Leon said softly. "Dehydration, yes. But you hadn't eaten in two days or slept properly. Fitch said you just lay there staring at nothing. He talked to you but you didn't hear him."

"And you said some things that worry me," Marek added gently. "That you could normally lock the pain away, but you couldn't this time, that you didn't feel right."

I slow blinked, the tiredness coming back to me like a wave. "I, uh . . ." I tried to swallow but my mouth was too dry. "I tried telling you both how I felt, how much I needed you. And you rejected me. I wasn't . . . My whole life I've been rejected, and I finally allowed myself to feel and dared to think you could want me . . ."

Leon put my hand to his lips. "I'm sorry about that. I'll forever be sorry about that. But we *do* want you. Marek and I talked it over, eventually, and we both admitted our feelings for you."

I looked at him, then at Marek. "You did?"

Marek smiled sadly. "I'll admit, I think my reaction was similar to yours in a lot of ways. To pull back, to retreat, to protect myself. Then after a day or two, we kind of yelled about it and the truth came out."

Hearing that made me both happy and sad. "I'm sorry I made you fight."

Leon let out a sigh. "We needed to clear the air as well. And then Fitch called us and it made everything clear. In that instant, we knew we had to go to you."

"I'm glad you did. I almost didn't believe it was really you," I said, trying to smile. "Thought my mind had finally cracked."

Marek held my hand in both of his. "Do you retreat into your mind a lot? To protect yourself?"

I stared at him, then at our joined hands, and conceded a nod. "I would do it when I was younger when . . . things were bad."

Leon closed his eyes slowly and Marek put my hand to his cheek.

"I don't talk about this," I said, the soup I'd eaten suddenly feeling a little off in my belly. "With anyone. Not even Fitch and Benji. It's not good for me."

"It's okay," Marek said. "You don't have to tell us now. Just whenever you're ready."

"Or with someone else," Leon murmured. "You can talk to a professional, if you'd prefer. If you're more comfortable. Whatever you want."

I'd rather not talk about it at all.

But it felt like a dam about to burst. Like one more setback and it would drag me under for good.

I let out a slow breath. "I want to talk about it but maybe not yet. I know I should. Probably. But . . ."

They both waited.

"My father wasn't a nice man," I began. "He'd lose his temper and . . ."

My stomach began to roll.

I licked my lips, trying to get the words out. "He would . . . the extension cord was his favourite . . ." I shook my head.

"Jesus Christ," Leon hissed.

"He caught me wearing my sister's skirt and . . ." I shook my head. "I'd locked the bathroom door so no one could see me, but he'd had a bad day . . ."

Marek sobbed and pulled me onto his lap. "My poor sweet boy," he whispered, over and over.

Leon kept his arms around us both, his arms trembling.

"I would disappear," I whispered. "Into my mind. And I could separate it all and lock it away."

Marek held me so damn tight and Leon rocked us back and forth, and I closed my eyes and let their strength surround me. Protect me.

I felt so small compared to them.

It was almost as if they were giants who scooped me up so the monsters couldn't reach me.

In my mind I pretended that's what they were, and I was their little one they'd protect and defend. No matter what I wore, no matter who I was.

And a part of my brain knew this wasn't healthy, this disassociation, and that maybe I should talk to a professional, like Leon had said. Maybe I would one day.

But today I'd said enough. I didn't want to rip open old wounds any more than I already had.

Not today.

I'd been through enough. I was drained enough.

"I feel safe with you," I said to them. "I'm safe here with you both, like this. In your arms, in your house. Nothing in the world can hurt me."

Leon pressed a kiss to the top of my head. "Never again. No one will ever hurt you again. And that includes me and us. I promise. I promise you both, I will do everything to make sure that doesn't happen."

Marek held my head to his chest, his thumping heart the most soothing sound. "We both will. The three of us together. I promise, Ky. And Leon, I promise you too."

I could have almost cried again.

They really were serious about this.

"How will it work? What does it mean?" I asked quietly.

Leon let us go, just enough so I could look up at him. "Well, that's what we need to discuss. Openly and honestly. About what we want and what we need from each other. If you even want it at all?"

If I even want it at all?

"Of course I do!" I whispered. "I will take whatever you give me."

"No, not whatever we give you," Marek said softly. "Sweet boy, you don't settle for anyone. Not even for us. You need to tell us what you want, what you need. As an equal. Not as an outsider, not as someone we invited in on occasion. Not anymore. You're one of us . . . if you decide it's what you want. No contract, no obligations, no anything. A relationship, a triangle, if you will, with three equal sides."

I looked up at him, then at Leon. "Really?"

Leon nodded. "Yes, b—"

Boy.

He was just about to call me boy.

Then there was that whole side of us.

Oh god.

"Am I still your boy?" I asked, my voice small. "Does it still include that? Are you still my daddies?"

Ah, shit.

Panic began to rise again . . .

"Because I don't know if I want this if you're not still my daddies. I want to be your boy. I need that—" Tears choked me up. "My skirts. My pretty . . . I need to feel pretty."

Marek took my face in his hands. "Oh, my darling boy," he murmured. "Whatever you want."

"Don't you want it too?" I asked. "Don't you need a boy as well?"

Leon let out a quiet, tormented sound. "Oh yes. We would be very happy with that."

"But do you need it? You keep saying what I want, what I need. What about you?"

"I need it," Leon said, his voice deep, rough. "I want it and I need it. If you're happy to continue that, then yes."

"I am," I said quickly. "I need it. You know I do."

Leon pressed a soft kiss to my forehead. "These are the things we need to talk about."

I nodded in agreement. "Okay."

"And your payments," Marek said.

My gaze shot to his. "Oh. Of course. Yeah, I don't expect that . . . I mean, if this is a relationship . . ." Of course they wouldn't continue to pay me if this was an actual relationship. Of course . . . "I don't need the money," I added quickly. "We're setting up the Only Fans and I'll need to make some more videos. I think Fitch wants to launch it soon, so we should start to see some money. Hopefully."

Marek smiled. "Good. That's fine with me. But there's no reason why you can't be our sugar baby. No more street work. The videos are fine. Solo work is more than fine. I hope you make serious money, but . . ."

"But?"

Oh god. There was a but.

"But we have enough money to support you," Marek said.

"For whatever you want," Leon added. "University? Law school? You're smart enough to make it happen, Ky. We'll support you in whatever you want."

Oh my god.

"Sugar daddies?" I said incredulously.

Like honestly, what?

Marek made a face. "It makes it sound bad. I just meant that we can support you. We don't want you to struggle when we have more than enough. I don't mean that we'd be paying you to stay with us. That's not what I meant." He looked to Leon for some help.

Leon smiled. "What Marek means to say is that you can take your time to decide what you want to do. You have financial stability, if you want, while you put your plans into action. If you want to go to university and forge a career, we can fund that. If you want to stay here and be a house boy in a silk robe and slippers all day, we would support that too. It's not about paying you, as Marek said, but about support." He looked around the room. "We have enough money, enough investments, to provide for the three of us several times over."

I couldn't believe what they were saying.

Marek took my hand, frowning. "I need to add something. I would also like to point out that sex is not a requirement, nor an obligation. That isn't part of this. If we agree to be in this relationship, we need to be clear from the start. Our previous agreement was based on sex and gratification, role playing. Relationships and growing together emotionally and sharing our lives is more than that. If sex is something we feel we can—"

"Okay, stop," I said, shaking my head. I was starting to feel a little overwhelmed. "I want what we had. I want all of what we used to have. I want to be your boy, I want you both to be my daddies, to have me however you want. We agreed all those months ago to make it a regular thing because it was fun and the sex was amazing, and the connection was intense. For the three of us. That doesn't have to change, does it? When I said I wanted more . . ."

I wasn't explaining this right.

"When you said you wanted more, what did you mean?" Leon asked.

"More. I just wanted . . . more of us." I looked at them both. "I see Benji with Nolan, and he's this huge emotional support pillar in his life now. And Fitch and Dominic . . . Dominic does things for him, they do things in public. And now with this court case coming, I know Nolan and Dominic will be there with them every step of the way. And I would be there alone. Because we had the NDA. We had an agreement that we could never be public, I could never discuss anything. I couldn't even tell them your names. And I understood why you insisted on it; you have professional reputations and careers, and I get that." I sighed. "At first the contract made me feel secure and the secrecy was fun. But then it felt like a shackle. I finally wanted to tell them how happy I was, but I couldn't. I wanted to talk about how amazing you both were, but I couldn't. I wanted you to be there for me . . ."

"But we couldn't," Marek finished quietly.

I nodded. "That's what I wanted. More of that. More normalcy, more honesty. A relationship, not an agreement. I was so close to finally being happy, finally feeling safe and secure and with two of the most amazing daddies ever, but I felt like I couldn't quite break the surface. I was drowning in it, and I needed something to change before it killed me."

Marek squeezed me and Leon rubbed my back, giving me all the time I needed to talk this through.

"I want sex," I said, looking at Marek. "Thank you for telling me I am under no obligation to provide that service, but I need you both to understand maybe you both have obligations to me?" I chuckled. "To fuck me thoroughly, to be my daddies, to help me be the prettiest femboy, one who makes his daddies happy and proud. That's what I need." I made a face. "If that's okay?"

Marek snorted and Leon laughed. "Oh, I think we can accommodate that."

I took a deep breath. "And thank you for the offer of supporting me, financially. That's something I will need to think about. And I know that's probably crazy to you, because it's insanely generous and I have nothing." Literally. "And being a houseboy in a silk robe and slippers sounds like a dream," I said, smiling at Leon. "The opportunity for university is . . . well, it's not something I ever thought possible, and maybe that's a way for me to finally contribute. Eventually. I don't know. I'll need some time to think about that."

I let out a long breath. *Here goes nothing.* "I still want

to do the solo videos with Fitch and Benji. And I don't expect you to understand my reasons. But I promised them. We made a pact years ago to stick together. They are my family, my brothers. And if that Only Fans account could be our way out, on our own terms, then I want to try. Not just for them, but for me too. We need to do this."

Leon put his arm around me. "I get it. You don't need to explain. Achieving financial security on your own is a huge deal. And I'm proud of you for giving it a shot."

I nodded quickly. "It'll all be anonymous, I promise. No face shots, nothing recognisable in the background." I'd told them all this before, when I'd first brought it up weeks ago, but I still felt the need to explain.

"It's more than that," Marek offered gently. "It's thinking about your future, setting goals, wanting better lives. Knowing you deserve a better life. Taking back control of your life."

I nodded, getting teary all over again.

He got it.

They both did, but Marek nailed it. "Yes. Exactly," I whispered. I felt so relieved, so blessed to have these two by my side. "Thank you, both of you. It all still feels kind of surreal."

Leon kissed the side of my head. "I know you're tired. We still have more to discuss, like living arrangements and public outings, what we tell people, if we tell them anything at all. Have a think about anything else you want to discuss, anything at all, and we can chat again once you've rested some more."

I was tired, that was true.

Marek felt my forehead again. "How are you feeling, sweetheart?"

"I feel so much better," I said. "Like the heaviest weight has been lifted off my shoulders. I'm so relieved and happy and grateful for you both."

But there was something that couldn't wait. Something I had to tell them.

"I just . . ." I sighed. "I need you both to know that I'm very happy to be included, to be part of your lives, and the fact you both love me is the best thing to ever happen to me. I just can't hardly believe it, to be honest. Like this is all some kind of dream I'll need to keep pinching myself to see if it's real."

"It's real, darling," Marek said, smiling.

"I just need you both to know . . ." I made a face. "Your marriage to each other, your vows to each other, I know I'm not part of that, but I need you both to know I respect that. More than anything."

They both stared at me, so I swallowed hard and tried again. "The fact you're married and so in love means the world to me. I mean fuck, you love each other so much you're willing to include me in your lives, and *that* means the world to me. I know I'm not explaining this correctly, but I just needed to acknowledge the fact you guys are married and I won't ever not recognise that." I put my hand to my forehead and laughed. "I don't even know what I'm trying to say. I just want you both to know that I understand there will be things inside your marriage that don't have to include me and that it's okay. What we have is our own, and I'm okay with that."

"Like grown-up daddy things?" Leon asked with a smile.

I swatted his arm. "Yes!" Then I shrugged. "Or something, I don't even know. I just need you both to know that I won't ever forget you are married. And it's not a bad thing. I don't feel excluded or left out. I actually love that you're married and look at each other with such adoration. It makes me feel . . . safer."

There. That was better.

Marek gave me a hug. "You're such a sweet boy."

"I love you both," I whispered. "And I know this won't be all sunshine and roses. But I will do my best to be everything you need."

Leon gave me a side hug and kissed my temple. "We just need you. The rest will work itself out."

"Are you tired, sweet boy?" Marek asked. "You're still not fully recovered."

I nodded. "I am tired still."

"Then lie down and rest."

"Will you lie with me?" I asked, looking at each of them. "Until I fall asleep?"

"Of course," Marek said.

I noticed then, like really noticed, just how tired they both looked as well. Leon scooped me up so Marek and I could use his arm as a pillow, and Marek faced me, his arm across my chest.

They'd lost sleep because of me. They'd fought and yelled at each other because of me.

They'd fought *for* me.

And lying there in that bed, in their arms, I felt something I'd never felt before.

I didn't know whether to laugh or cry.

"What is it, sweetheart?" Marek asked.

I let out a teary laugh. "This feeling. I just realised what this is. It feels like flying and floating and somersaults and swooping in my belly. It's scary and wonderful, and I've never . . . I've never felt anything like it. Not from anyone. Not my family, not even Fitch and Benji. I love them, but this . . . this is like nothing I've ever felt."

They both nuzzled in closer. Leon kissed my temple. "It's love, Kylan."

I nodded, a few happy tears forming but I didn't want to cry anymore. I was done crying.

"I don't know why I'm crying. I haven't cried this much since I was very little. I don't like crying. All these feelings . . ."

Leon pulled me in close and Marek sandwiched me, wrapping me up snug and safe.

"You're allowed to cry," Leon murmured. "You don't have to lock down how you feel anymore."

Marek looked so damn sad. "You're allowed to feel. And it's okay to be overwhelmed at first. You're not used to being so vulnerable, and that's scary. But darling, you'll be okay. I promise."

I nodded again. "Thank you."

And the truth was, this emotional dump was an ugly onslaught. I'd struggled my whole life in keeping a lid on my emotions, tamping them down, until I felt nothing at all.

And now I was surrounded, blanketed by such raw and honest love.

It was so foreign to me and overwhelming, like Leon had said.

And that was the thing . . . they understood. They knew. When I was reeling, out of control and aimless like a kite in the wind, while they were calm and in control, keeping me tethered. Not afraid to admit their fears and being vulnerable with me and ensuring that I felt safe.

The perfect daddies.

I had so much to process. So much to take in and so many questions to ask.

So much to learn.

But for now, all I wanted to do was sleep. Be cradled by these two men who loved me. Let myself be loved.

And, if I could ever be brave enough, love them as much in return.

TEN
MAREK

KYLAN WAS EXHAUSTED.

He was physically and emotionally wiped out, dehydrated, and under nourished.

He didn't need hospitalisation or even a doctor.

The fact he was drinking and eating, and passing urine, was reassuring enough that we could manage that on our own. We could ensure his body received the right nutrients and adequate hydration and enough rest.

What we couldn't do was fix the lifetime of neglect and abuse he'd suffered at the hands of his family, his father.

Sure, we could safeguard him, make sure he knew he was safe and loved, protected. And, moving forward, that was great.

But we couldn't repair the damage that was done. Not on our own.

He was going to need professional help for that. Help

that we could encourage and pay for, but it was Kylan who needed to take that first step.

All we could do was hold his hands and gently steer him in the right direction. We couldn't make him get help. We couldn't make him do anything.

There was no contract, no obligations to be met on a legal basis. This was a relationship now, not a clause in a binding agreement.

After we'd all had a much-needed nap, Kylan wanted to venture downstairs. He needed a change of scenery, and his room was beginning to feel too small.

He wanted to cuddle up with us on the sofa and watch a movie—with him in the middle, of course—which was perfect, and to be honest, something the three of us needed.

We needed to feel connected while also being very normal.

If normal was something we ever were . . .

While being very much boyfriends.

Because maybe that is what we all were?

I still wasn't sure . . .

"Can I ask something?" Kylan asked. The movie was clearly not holding his attention.

"Sure," Leon replied.

"Will you tell me about your families?" he asked. "What your personal lives are like? Where you grew up, that kind of thing. I realised I don't know anything about that. Is that something I should know?"

I chuckled. "Of course, darling. My parents are here in Sydney. My mother was born in France, and she met my father when he travelled to Europe after college."

"Oh, how romantic," he whispered. "And Leon? What about you?"

"My father passed away sixteen years ago," he said. "My mother remarried. They live on the northern beaches."

Kylan nodded eagerly.

"I have one brother," Leon added. "And Marek has four siblings."

He shot me a look. "Four?"

I chuckled. "Yes. Two brothers, two sisters."

"And they . . . they know you're gay?" Kylan made a face. "I mean, you're married, so I guess they do."

"Do you mean are they okay with it?" Leon asked.

"I guess."

"Sure," I replied with a shrug. "Not that it would have mattered either way. Because the day I met Leon, I knew I was going to spend my life with him."

Kylan's whole face lit up and he wiggled happily. "Tell me about how you met."

I laughed and shook my head. "Well, we met when we were at university, as you know," I answered. "It was a block party and I was drunk and dancing with another guy."

Kylan giggled and nodded for me to continue.

"And in walked this absolutely gorgeous man. Tall, confident, stunning. I couldn't take my eyes off him."

"I was also very sober," Leon added. "I'd just finished work. I walked in and there he was—tight jeans, shirt unbuttoned, cute moustache—slutting it up with another man."

Kylan was grinning now. "And what did you do?"

Leon looked at me when he answered. "I walked over and kissed him."

"When he was dancing with another guy?"

"Absolutely. I thought that *right there is the man I am going to marry*."

Kylan swooned, so enthralled. "So what happened with the other guy?"

"Oh, we fucked him good and proper that night," I answered.

Kylan laughed and clapped his hands. "That's perfect."

"And a few more nights that year, if I remember correctly," Leon said, his eyes on mine.

I chuckled, because of course he remembered correctly.

"So you've always been into threesomes?" Kylan asked.

"Pretty much." I nodded. "I do bottom, occasionally, but I don't love it. I don't crave it." Then I made a face. "I'm better at topping."

"Yes, you are," Kylan agreed.

That made me chuckle. "We've always invited a third into our beds. Usually someone smaller that we could pass between us, manhandle easily. We were just always drawn to twinks and pretty femboys."

Leon hummed. "Then, about fifteen years ago, we

met a twink at a bar. He called us daddy, and that unlocked a new set of doors for us."

Kylan made a contented sound. "Thank you bartwink for paving the way for me."

That made me laugh. "So yes, to answer your question, yes, we've always had a third. Very rarely a repeat though. We did have a contract in place with another man, maybe five years ago now?"

I looked at Leon and he nodded.

"What happened to him?" Kylan asked, frowning now.

"He met someone," I replied, smiling at the fond memory. "He was a barista. Liked a bit of kink. Loved the toys, loved having two daddies."

"But then he met another man," Leon added. "And that was that. We were happy for him. He was . . . he was fun. I suggested the NDA because the café he worked at was in the legal district. He met a lot of our colleagues and associates."

Kylan nodded. "Sounds fair."

"And I thought," Leon added with a sigh, "when we agreed to have you on a regular basis that we should have some sort of similar arrangement. I didn't realise how it would make you feel."

Kylan shook his head. "And I didn't either. Like I said, at first I liked it. But then I didn't."

"We're glad you told us," I said. "Anything you're not comfortable with, you need to let us know."

"I won't ever tell anyone anything about us anyway,"

Kylan added. "I know that doesn't mean much in a legal sense. But I won't ever betray you. If someone ever asks me anything—about what I wear for you, about the toys we use, the names we use—I'll tell them I don't know what they're talking about." He shrugged. "Well, probably except Fitch. He's a total whore for details. Explicit details. But he knows not to tell anyone. It's a hooker code. Never snitch."

Leon took Kylan's hand and smiled with a quiet sigh. "I know you won't. I trust you."

"I do too," I chimed in. "Though we should probably work out what we're going to tell people. When we go to family functions or to work events. We'll need to have our stories straight because you know people *will* ask."

Kylan's wide eyes met mine. "Family functions? Work events?" He shook his head. "Uh, I don't know about that. I don't know if I . . . When I said I wanted us to be more public, I was thinking maybe dinner with Fitch or Benji, and Dominic and Nolan, of course. Or coffee at a café. Something much more low-key than family gatherings and work events."

Leon chuckled. "You don't have to do anything you're not comfortable with. And maybe we should give him some time to acclimate before he meets your sisters," he said, smiling at me. "But yes, we should devise a plan of action for what to tell people."

"You could tell them I'm a nephew or something," Kylan offered. "Or a long-lost child from some experimental hook-up with a woman."

I barked out a laugh. "Or we could go with something a little more honest."

"Such as?" Kylan whispered.

"That you're our boyfriend?" I looked at Leon to see what he thought, and he smiled.

"I'm happy with that."

"Boyfriend?" Kylan looked stunned and a little bewildered, truth be told.

"Is that not okay?" I asked him.

He let out a high-pitched laugh. "Uh, yes! I just didn't think . . . I wasn't sure if that's . . . Is that what I am? A boyfriend?"

I gestured between myself and Leon. "Husband." Then I pointed to him. "Boyfriend."

Kylan nodded and laughed all at once, his hand to his forehead. "This is crazy. Can I call Fitch? I should probably check in anyway, but he's gonna freak out."

"Of course you can," Leon said. "You don't need to ask permission."

Kylan leaned over and kissed his cheek. "Thank you, daddy," he said, then shot up off the sofa and raced upstairs.

Leon blushed, and damn, if it wasn't the cutest thing ever. I took Kylan's place and snuggled into Leon. "We're going to be okay."

Leon gave me a squeeze. "Yeah, I think we will."

BECAUSE WE WEREN'T GOING into work the next day, we had a late breakfast with an agenda for the day of doing not much at all.

Kylan had slept in his bed alone last night.

After dinner, Leon had suggested he get a good night's sleep so he woke up feeling a hundred percent tomorrow.

Kylan didn't love the idea, but he still needed to rest and recover, and he needed to know that this new arrangement was more than just sex.

It was also nice for me and Leon to spend the night sleeping in each other's arms. We needed to reconnect too. Not in a sexual way but in a closeness, been-together-for-twenty-five-years kind of way.

But by mid-afternoon, after lingering hugs and his need to be close and touching us, I could tell Kylan was more than just bored. He was uncomfortable. As if he wanted to ask us something but was unsure how.

He'd eaten well, he'd drank a lot of water and juice, he said he felt great.

"Come here, darling," I said. I pulled him onto my lap, and he was quick to lean in, his head against my neck. "Is something on your mind?"

He was quiet for a long moment that told me yes, something was on his mind.

"I know daddy said I need to recover," he murmured.

As soon as he'd used the word daddy, I knew where this was going.

He squirmed a little. "And I know daddy knows best."

I rubbed his back. "Yes, we want you to be back to your old self, darling."

He squirmed again. "I feel fine, daddy. I feel like . . ."

"Like what, sweetheart?" I soothed, rocking him a little.

"Like I'd feel so much better if you fucked me." He arched his back a little, squirming still. "I think I need it, daddy. I need you both to have me. I need you to prove to me that I'm yours. Please, daddy?"

I hummed.

We'd wondered how long we should leave it until we broached the subject with him. We needed to show patience and restraint while he made the decision about what he needed.

I guess he'd just made his mind up.

"Will daddy mind?" Kylan asked, his eyes wide with innocence. "I don't want him to get mad or tell me no because he thinks I'm not feeling better. But daddy, I am," he said. Then he palmed his crotch and winced. "I can't stop thinking about it."

I put my finger to his chin and pulled his face up. "Go upstairs and get yourself ready. I'll go talk to daddy."

Because I knew Leon, and I knew that he wanted the same thing. He wanted to celebrate this new stage in our relationship. He'd wanted to take Kylan into our bed last night, but he'd said Kylan needed the rest. That he'd needed time to adjust and to feel safe with us without the presumption of sex.

But he'd wanted him.

The same way I'd wanted him. But Leon was right. We had to let Kylan take the lead and be the one to tell us when he was ready.

Which he'd just done.

I watched Kylan disappear up the stairs, then went to find Leon in his office. He'd had a few emergency business things to take care of, but he'd been gone a while.

The door was ajar and I could see him at his desk, sitting back in his chair, staring at some papers on his desk. I lightly knocked, startling him. "Hey," I said, walking in.

He smiled at me. "Hey."

I walked around to his side of the desk, swivelled his desk chair around, and sat on his lap. He slung one arm around my waist, the other resting on my knee. "You looked lost in thought. Everything okay?"

He hummed and picked up the papers, handing them to me.

It was the NDA we'd all signed.

"Oh."

"Should we sign a release statement?" he asked. "Or just tear it up?"

I sighed. "Maybe we should ask Kylan."

He nodded, looking up at me and smiling. "Where is he?"

I laughed. "Well, about that . . ."

ELEVEN

KYLAN

I WANTED this to be perfect.

I took all the time I needed to make sure I was properly ready. Cleaned out, scrubbed clean, a spritz of body mist, a touch of lip gloss.

Some frilly panties under a flowy, tiered, very short pink skirt. No shirt, but a long pink beaded necklace. And I wrapped one around my wrist for a bracelet as well.

And my favourite vibrating butt plug, doused in lube and set to pulse while I got dressed.

I was so ready for this.

I needed this.

And I needed them to not have to wait. To not hold back. I needed them to fill me and fuck me, to own me however they dared.

I needed them to show me what I meant to them. What this *relationship* was.

What it could be.

There was so much unknown territory ahead of us and I needed something familiar. Comforting.

And that was me, in the middle of them.

I switched the butt plug off, letting the absence of sensations settle through me. With a belly full of nerves, I took one last look at myself in the mirror—smiling at who I saw smiling back at me—and opened my door.

And stopped.

Marek and Leon were waiting in the hallway.

Leon leaning against the wall, head turned my way, eyes dark as onyx. A very prominent bulge in his jeans.

Oh god.

Marek was closer. He smiled at me, licking the corner of his mouth. "Oh, princess," he whispered. "You look so beautiful. Do a full turn for us. Let us see you."

A rush of warmth flooded through me, my skin feeling flushed and tingly. I went to my tiptoes, touched the beads on my chest, and turned around. When I had my back to them, I slid my skirt up so they could see what I'd done for them.

When I turned back to face them, Marek's nostrils were flared and Leon pushed off the wall. "You are so pretty," he said, voice low and gruff. "So perfect."

He came to stand alongside Marek, and I handed Leon the remote control. "For you, daddy."

He grunted as he took it, and while they both watched me, he pressed the On button.

Jolts of pleasure seared through me and I gasped, my hands flailing before I could control my reaction.

I was so high-strung, so turned on.

Marek held his hand out for me to take. "Does that feel good, princess?"

I nodded, not trusting my voice at first. The urge to arch my back, to claw at the walls was strong. "Yes, daddy," I said, voice strained.

Leon held out his hand for me, and they led me into their bedroom. They both turned to me and I felt so small, so in awe of them, how big they were, how strong.

"Are you sure this is what you want?" Marek whispered, his finger tracing the beads up my torso. "Tell us how you feel."

"I feel . . . I feel close. I feel safe and happy, but also a little . . . adrift. Everything ahead of me is unknown and I'm excited but I also need something familiar. I need you both to show me, remind me. I need you both. That's where I feel safest. That's where I feel the most loved."

Leon hummed, almost a tortured sound. "I need you too," he said, pulling me against him. His hands covered my back, my arse.

Marek stepped in behind me, sandwiching me.

The way I fucking loved it.

Leon pressed the vibrator up a level and I cried out, but they held me firm. Surrounded me, encased me with their bodies, their hands. I could feel their erections, how much they wanted me, how much they needed me.

If pleasure was a fire, then I damned near fucking burned.

Marek held my hips and ground his erection against my arse, against the butt plug. "I can feel the vibrations," he said. "Fuck."

"Please, daddy," I murmured. "I need you both. I need you both to have me. Own me, show me, please."

Leon grunted, raked his hand through the back of my hair, and pulled my head back so he could crush his mouth to mine.

Hot, demanding, invading.

Perfect.

And the way Marek was holding my hips, his erection pressed firm against the butt plug . . . it was heaven.

"Let me taste," Marek said.

Leon turned me around, quickly grinding his cock against my arse while Marek plundered his tongue into my mouth. I was on edge, my balls so heavy, my cock hard.

Then Leon went to his knees behind me. He lifted my skirt, pulled my panties to one side, and inspected the butt plug. He hummed, tapping it a few times, wiggling it, and I cried out into Marek's kiss.

Marek held me strong and chuckled. "Such a good boy. Is it too much?"

I nodded. Because it was. Sensation overload. But somehow . . . "Too much," I breathed. "Not enough."

Then the butt plug stopped vibrating and Leon pulled it out. I gasped and clung to Marek. He held me tight, supporting me. And Leon spread my arse cheeks and hummed.

"Such a beautiful gape," he murmured. Then he inserted his tongue into my hole.

I went up onto my toes, clinging to Marek, moaning

as Leon ate my arse. "Oh god, daddy," I cried, my voice high, strung tight.

Marek chuckled, warm and throaty in my ear. "Save some for me," he said.

Leon removed his tongue and kissed up my spine, gently nipping the skin on my shoulder. "He got himself ready for us," Leon said. Then he took my hand and led me to kneel on the bed. "Spread yourself wide so daddy can taste you."

I was flush all over, ready and so fucking willing.

I leaned forward, offering my arse, and Marek spread my cheeks and tasted me.

Ate me.

"Fuck, that's hot," Leon murmured.

"Daddy," I whined. "Need your cock in me."

Leon crawled onto the bed and positioned himself in front of me. "Take daddy's cock out," he said.

I couldn't get it out fast enough. So thick and hard, scent of arousal strong.

Intoxicating.

"Good boy," he whispered. "Now suck it."

I took him straight in deep, sucking hard and fast. He fisted my hair and hissed, and then Marek's mouth was gone from my arse, soon replaced by the head of his cock.

This is what I needed.

This is what I craved.

Marek pushed into me, long and deep in one slow thrust. "Oh god," he said, breath hitching. "Pretty boy feels so good."

"Look at how he takes both of us," Leon said, fucking my mouth. "He was made for us."

I pulled off Leon's cock. "Both of you."

Those words were out before I'd registered them, but it was what I wanted.

No. It was what I *needed.*

Leon took my chin in his hand and drew me up. It changed the angle Marek was hitting and I whined as Leon kissed me.

"You are so beautiful like this," Leon said, his eyes dark. "In your pretty skirt with daddy's cock buried in your arse. I love how you love it."

And holy fuck, did I love this . . .

"I want you both," I said. I was fast approaching that happy place, that place of bliss where nothing else existed. Getting railed by one while the other held me and praised me.

But I wanted them both.

"Inside me," I said. "At the same time. Both of you. I need it."

Leon stared and Marek stopped fucking me, his hands stilling my hips.

"You want us to DP you?" Leon asked. His eyes were intense and deadly serious. "You told us before you didn't think that was for you."

"And now I need it," I said. "Please, daddy. Please say yes. Please. If you want me to beg . . ."

He groaned, and he and Marek had some silent conversation above my head.

"Are you sure, baby doll?" Marek asked.

"You said if I wanted something, I should ask, and now I'm asking and you deny me," I said, surprised by how emotional I was. This was desperation and—

Marek pulled out of me.

"No," I cried, turning to look at him. "Don't pull out, I need you—"

He was quick to pull me close, holding me to his chest. "Okay, baby," he crooned. "You need this so bad, huh?"

I nodded, about to tell him just how bad I needed it when I realised that Leon was getting into position. Lying on the bed propped up by the pillows, his erect cock ready, waiting.

"Be a good boy," Marek said. "And sit on daddy's cock."

Leon held his hand out for me, which I took. "Come here, princess."

He held my hand as I positioned his cock at my hole.

"Wait," Marek said. "Let me add more lube."

"I already did that," I said, needing them to know I was a good boy.

"You'll need more," Leon said. "We don't want to hurt you."

While Marek slicked us all up, I tried to clear my mind.

I wanted this. I needed this so fucking bad. I expected the stretch, the burn. I was prepared for that. Because if it meant they were in me together, then I was more than willing.

"Okay, baby doll," Marek murmured. "Daddy's ready for you. You can tell us at any time to stop, and we will."

I nodded, and with Leon holding my hands, I sank down on his hard cock. He was big, and most of the time he fucked me after Marek because then I was adequately stretched for him, so I knew taking both was going to be a lot . . .

The butt plug had stretched me, Marek's cock had stretched me, and Leon felt so good . . . the way he gritted his teeth, the way his nostrils flared. The way he kept completely still . . .

His self-control turned me on.

Marek pushed my shoulders down and Leon quickly put his arms around me.

This was my favourite position. One of them holding me while the other fucked me . . .

But now I was about to take both.

Marek shuffled in behind me, rubbing my back. "Take a deep breath, sweetheart," he said.

Then he was pushing for entry.

My body recoiled because there was no way, no way I could take them both.

But Leon held me still, his strong arms around me, his gentle voice in my ear. "You can take us," he whispered. "Take both your daddies, just like you wanted. I know you can."

Marek had one hand on my back, one gripping my hip, and he pushed in. The breach was too much. They were too big, too much. I cried out, the need to tell them to stop was on the tip of my tongue.

But then I saw Leon's face.

The pleasure, the intensity, the wonder.

His nostrils flared, his neck corded with restraint, his body trembling. He looked fraught with pleasure, his mouth open in surprise.

And to know that I'd made this big strong man lose his composure, that I'd made him look like that. That I'd brought him pleasure like that . . .

I forgot my own pain for a minute.

And then Marek began to move, to control our bodies, and there was no pain at all.

I was so full. I was so open.

Both their cocks sliding in a tug of war of pleasure.

"Oh fuck," Leon cried, his fingers digging into my hips. "I need to come already. Fuck, Marek your cock feels so good. Kylan, baby. You're so fucking perfect."

Then Marek wrapped an arm around my chest, forcing me to lean back, forcing the angles to change. Forcing me to shudder and cry out.

Forcing Leon to come.

His back arched, rigid and straining, his hands gripping me, pulling me onto him while he drove his cock up . . .

Pulsing and shooting his load so fucking deep.

Marek groaned and bucked his hips, swelling and surging; he came with a roar like I'd never heard from him.

I felt every throb, every gush of his come, filling me.

Completing me.

Leon groaned as he slipped out of me, but Marek

stayed buried, pushing me down onto Leon, and he lay on top of me. Leon's chest rose and fell with ragged breaths and Marek was a delicious heavy weight on me.

Leon's hands cupped my face, cradled my head, and kissed my forehead, murmuring sweet nothings.

Marek was still catching his breath, still inside me. "Our beautiful boy," he whispered. "How do you feel?"

"Floaty," I answered. "And full. I could stay like this forever."

Leon took my face and pulled me up, straining to kiss me. "You are a gift," he said. "What you have given us tonight is a gift."

Marek pushed up, kissing the nape of my neck. His cock in me felt sublime. Marek's weight, Leon's arms, his body my pillow. I was stretched and filled and slick with their seed.

Full of their love.

Marek hummed and rolled his hips. "I want to stay in you forever," he mumbled, nosing the back of my head. "Both of us inside you, so fucking good. You were made for us, beautiful boy."

But then he pulled back, slowly slipping out of me. I whined at the loss, and Leon rolled us onto our sides. Marek fell in behind me and the three of us cuddled, entwined.

Leon tilted my chin up and pressed a soft kiss to my lips. "Do you feel okay?"

I nodded. "Oh, yes, daddy."

"Was it what you hoped it would be?" Marek asked, nuzzling into the back of my head.

"Everything and more," I replied. "I don't know if I'll be able to do it often, but I *do* want to do it again. I want to experience this again. Every time I need reminding, or every time I need to feel connected."

They held me tighter, and Leon hummed. "Whatever you want, baby doll."

I preened and sighed happily. "Call me that again."

They both chuckled. "Baby doll," Leon whispered.

"Beautiful baby doll," Marek said. He raked his hand up my side, giving me the urge to stretch like a cat. "What do you want? A hot bath? A shower? Name it and we'll make it happen. Whatever you want."

"I want . . ." I tried to think. "I want nothing right now. Nothing but this right here."

And that was the very truth.

"Promise me we'll have this," I said, sleepy and happy. "This is all I want."

"We promise," Marek murmured, half asleep.

Leon had his eyes closed, his arms around us both. "Promise, baby doll."

———

I WALKED into our tiny apartment and Fitch stuck his head out of his room. "Thought I heard you." He came out to meet me. "How are you? You look . . ." He studied me. "You look good."

I cracked a smile. "I am. Never been better, actually. And I have you to thank."

His smile became a grin. "Holy fuck. You look . . .

happy. What the fuck happened? I want every detail. All the feels and all the filth."

That made me laugh, which clearly struck something in Fitch. His face lit up.

"You owe me the filthiest details and I will accept nothing less." Then his smile died. "Oh, your contract. If you can't . . ."

"Null and void," I said. "We are released from the NDA."

He grabbed my arm. "Okay. I was about to go get my kink on for the camera, but this is so much better. Tell me everything. Names, details, cock size. What it's like to get to have two smoking hot daddies. I've seen them, I know they're hot. I bet the one with the moustache is the kinky one, right? And the other one is the daddiest daddy, amiright? I totally got that vibe. I want the porniest details. All of it. Spare no filth."

I chuckled.

He narrowed his eyebrows at me. "Kylan, I'm not kidding. I'm glad you feel better. I'm glad you three clearly sorted shit out. But I've been deprived of the details for months. You bought all those vibrating butt plugs and whatnot, so I know the sex is fun and hot and amazing, and you gotta give me something."

I laughed again. "Okay. Only because I owe it all to you for calling them. Take a seat, you filthy pervert. I'll tell you everything."

TWELVE
LEON

KYLAN STAYED the whole next day and the three of us rarely left each other's side. We cared for him after the double penetration. He said he wasn't too sore, just a twinge or two, but he was clingier than normal.

We all were.

I'd partaken in my share of DPs over the years—Marek and I had invited many thirds into our bed in the last two decades—but this was different.

This felt surreal. Intense, pleasure like nothing I'd ever felt. And it solidified something that we already knew.

We were now three.

For real.

And for always.

We'd dropped Kylan back to his place on our way to work the morning after. He hadn't made any decisions yet—about what he wanted to do about living arrangements or university. Or anything, really—but he was happy.

And that was all we wanted.

For now, at least.

He could take all the time he needed to make sure it was the best decision for him.

"Do you think he'll move in with us?" Marek gave me a sad look as I drove us to work. "I want him to, and I know you do too."

I reached over and gave his thigh a squeeze. "Of course I do. And I think yes, he will. But it needs to be his decision. We can't rush him."

"His apartment is . . ."

Terrible. Small. Grungy. Old.

"His apartment is his," I allowed. "We can't separate him from his friends. They have a unique bond. They've been through a lot together."

He sighed. "I know. Maybe we could call Dominic and plant some little seeds about Fitch moving in with him, and then Ky will have to move in."

"Marek," I admonished.

He sighed again. "Fine. But if he is determined to stay in that place, the least we could do is buy the entire apartment complex and upgrade it. He wouldn't have to know it was us. He'd have secure housing then, and I wouldn't have to worry."

I chuckled at him. "Why not just buy the whole block?"

He shot me a look. "Don't think I'm joking, darling."

"Oh, I know you're not."

He sniffed, and after a moment of silence, his tone was sombre. "Though we do need to speak to Dominic. And Nolan. Now we know who Benji is."

I sighed and conceded a nod. "Yes. Yes, we do."

When Kylan had mentioned attending Benji's pending court case, I'd not said anything, but I knew Marek had earmarked it too. When we were talking more last night, he'd told us who his friend really was.

He'd claimed he didn't know details until recently, and I believed him.

But every lawyer in Sydney knew the name Barbieri. Hell, anyone who saw the news, read a newspaper, or worked in any legal setting knew who Bruno Barbieri was.

And that his son had gone missing some years ago.

Except he hadn't.

Now, our expertise was property law, not criminal, not public prosecutions, but we knew damn well who Benji was.

It was big news.

And these three boys were caught up in the centre of it all.

Not that I believed Kylan was in any immediate danger, but he had been involved in a police sting to nab the two men chasing Benji.

Dominic and Nolan were lucky we hadn't known when it was going down.

I wouldn't have allowed Kylan to be used as bait like that, and it surprised me that Dominic and Nolan had.

Until Kylan reminded me that they were grown men

who could make their own decisions and didn't need permission.

He reminded me that the daddy/boy line was a tightrope to navigate, and sometimes instead of saying our boy couldn't walk the tightrope should he fall, it was more our duty to hold his hand while he walked it.

And while the daddy in me wanted to wrap him up in cotton wool and protect him at all costs, I knew there would be times when he had to stand on his own two feet.

"I'm not sure I can be in boy mode twenty-four seven," he'd said. "Sometimes I'll need some downtime. Just time to decompress and be me. It's hard because as soon as I see you both, I automatically slip into boy mode. I want to kneel at your feet or curl up in your arms. I want you to praise me and call me pretty. It's like something switches in my brain and I love it. You know I love it. But I don't know how healthy that would be for me long term. I want to be in this forever, and I don't want to risk burning out."

"Hey, sweet boy," Marek had replied gently. "We don't know how to do this long term either. We're learning together, okay? That's what relationships are. Learning and growing together. We can just play it all by ear, see how we feel as we go along, make changes as necessary, okay?"

Kylan was much happier after that, and I understood his reticence. I understood his hesitance, his reluctance.

Did I want him to move in and be our boy twenty-four seven?

At first, I'd thought yes, of course I did.

But then I realised what Kylan was saying was right. We would all need some downtime. No pressure for us to be in daddy mode every waking minute.

We could just be ourselves, delving into the daddy and sweet boy role playing when it suited all three of us. I had the feeling it would be most nights he stayed with us. But it would be okay if it wasn't *every* time.

We had to learn his cues and meet his needs, and it was a daddy's job to understand the difference of a boy needing his daddies or a man needing his partners.

We would learn together.

"I'm not saying I will buy his entire apartment complex," Marek said. I had to wonder what part of his musings I'd missed . . . "But perhaps we could look at the person who does own it and see if they have any prior violations for not updating to code."

I laughed. "Marek, stop. Leave him be. I do believe he'll move in with us eventually. Just let him get used to the idea."

Marek huffed and pouted, his moustache twitching. Then he let out a sigh. "When should we tell our families?"

"I don't know. Let's just get used to the idea first. It's all new. And when, or if, Kylan moves in, then we can figure out what to say."

"My sister's birthday dinner is coming up," he mused out loud.

I snorted. "Please tell me you won't subject Kylan to

that kind of torture. God, please tell me you won't subject *me* to that kind of torture."

He put his hand to his chest. "I don't even want to go." Then he sighed again. "Though the look on my sister's face would be priceless."

I took his hand and brought his knuckles to my lips. "Don't be mean to your sister."

My phone rang and I saw the name on the dash screen. Our phones rang a lot. The majority of our calls were business related, but this one was personal.

I hit Answer. "Ah, Dominic," I said. "We were just talking about you."

"Oh?"

"Just that we should call you," I added. "You're on speaker, by the way. It's just Marek and I in the car, and this traffic is dreadful."

"Hello, darling," Marek said.

"Good morning to you both." He paused for a second. "I take it things with Ky went well? Fitch told me he called you. He was very worried."

I smiled. "It went well, yes. And I appreciate Fitch calling us. It was the kick in the pants we needed."

"Your Fitch is a tenacious one," Marek said. "He had no qualms whatsoever in telling us what he thought."

Dominic laughed. "Yes, tenacious indeed." Then he paused again. "I just spoke to Fitch, actually. He told me he and Ky were at the unit."

"Yes, we just dropped him off," I said. "Dominic, is everything okay? If you have something to say in regard to Kylan—"

"No, not at all," he replied quickly. "It's just that he . . . well, I guess you both and Ky sorted things out and Fitch mentioned that things were no longer tied to an NDA."

I looked at Marek. "Yes, that's correct. Why?"

Dominic sighed. "Well, Fitch decided that maybe it would be a good idea if we had a dinner. All of us. I don't know if you know that Nolan's boy Benji has a pretty big court appearance coming up, and Fitch thought it'd be nice to get together beforehand. And once Fitch decides something . . . well, that's the end of that. Like you said, tenacious. Anyway, he said Ky has to be there and I needed to call you to, and I quote, 'word you up.'"

I chuckled. "Are you inviting us to dinner, Dominic?"

"Yes. The three of you."

Marek grinned at me. "Just tell us when and where."

SO OUR FIRST social outing with the three of us as a throuple was going to Dominic's house four nights later.

It was a casual, low-key affair, but it was the perfect opportunity to test the waters.

To test how we'd navigate social settings and relationship dynamics. And these were Kylan's two best friends, so he was safe and free to be himself.

So I was surprised when he came down from his room wearing jeans and a shirt.

"No skirt tonight?" I asked.

He trotted over to me and quickly put his arm around

my waist, his face into my chest. "No." Then he looked up at me, eyes bright and cheeks pink, his lips with a hint of gloss. "I think I want to wear skirts here for you and daddy and no one else. I wore one at home yesterday and Fitch didn't care. I was comfortable, but it wasn't the same. When I wear a skirt for you and daddy, it's special. You treat me special, and I want it to stay just for us. Is that okay?"

My heart grew another size, full to bursting. I leaned down and pressed a soft kiss to his lips. "Of course it is. I like that it's special, and I like that you only want to do it for us. But whatever you want, princess. You're still our baby doll, no matter what you wear."

He smiled so serenely. "I love you, daddy," he whispered. Then he chewed on his bottom lip. "Well, I wore a skirt in the video I made yesterday."

"You did, huh?"

He nodded, taking out his phone. "Wanna watch it, daddy?"

I laughed and stopped him. "Ah, no, not right now. If I watch that, we won't be going to Dominic's. Maybe we can save it for when we get home?"

Kylan grinned and nodded, even wiggling a little. "Yessss."

"What are we saving for when we get home?" Marek asked as he came downstairs. He looked dashing in his charcoal trousers, purple button-down shirt, and grey waistcoat. His moustache was expertly shaped to neat little points, and he had a twinkle in his eye.

Kylan opened his arm for Marek to join us. "My

latest video," Kylan answered. "Daddy said we can watch it later. If we watch it now, he said we won't make it to dinner."

Marek hummed. It had been three days since we'd had sex, and my balls were reminding me that we needed to remedy that.

I had to readjust my dick, and I bit back a groan. "We need to not even talk about watching that video and what we'll be doing after. Christ."

Kylan giggled and snuggled up to Marek. "Daddy's gonna give it to me so good when we get home."

"Okay, that's enough or we won't be going anywhere," I said, trying to be stern but also needing to readjust myself again. At this rate I'd be going to this dinner party with a raging hard-on.

Or we wouldn't be going anywhere but to the bedroom.

"Don't forget the wine, darling," Marek said. He and Kylan were heading toward the hall with an arm around each other.

I grabbed the wine bottle off the kitchen counter and smiled as I followed them to the car.

The ride over was peaceful, pleasant even. I drove with Marek in the passenger seat, as per usual. Kylan sat in the back, as he usually did when we picked him up or dropped him home, but this time felt different.

I kept one eye on the road, the other on my rear-vision mirror, on him. He was smiling as he texted, took a selfie, and grinned at the replies. I guessed it was Fitch and/or Benji, and it made me smile.

Marek slid his hand onto my thigh, smiling at me.

We were so freaking happy. I couldn't have ever imagined I'd love Marek more, but I did. I loved Kylan the same, and it surprised me still that I could love so much.

We'd never been to Dominic's house before. In the fading evening daylight, with the warm glow of lights inside and picture-perfect street appeal, it gave me a warm family vibe that I wanted for us too.

"Everything okay?" Marek asked as he joined me on the footpath outside.

"Yes, never better," I replied. "Just questioning the sudden desire to do the nuclear-family thing, picket-fence, yard-with-a-dog thing."

Marek stared at me, stunned, then let out an odd laugh. "Oh dear."

Kylan appeared in front of us and he levelled a glare at me. "Nuclear family implies two children and there's only enough room for one. I am an only child here, and I will not share my daddies."

The seriousness, the outburst from our quiet little submissive boy was quite the shock.

Marek laughed, as stunned as me. "Right, then." Then he turned to me. "He has spoken."

Then Kylan sniffed. "The dog, on the other hand, I'm not opposed to."

I took his chin between my thumb and forefinger, smiling. "Only child, huh?"

Just then, Dominic's front door opened and Fitch appeared. "Kysie, you get that perfect arse of yours in this house right now," he said, coming down the path to grab Kylan's hand. He paused long enough to meet our gazes before he dragged Kylan into the house.

Then Dominic was there, holding the door for us. Apparently, Fitch dragging someone into his house wasn't surprising to him. "Please, come in."

"Thank you," I said, walking inside.

Marek handed him the bottle of wine and we walked in together. His house was lovely, very homely, warm tones, subdued and sensible furnishings.

Nolan was in the kitchen fixing a bowl of something, and three boys stood by the sofa. They stood close together, touching, leaning into each other, all eyes on us.

As our first social outing together, I reminded myself, it was an announcement of sorts, an introduction as Kylan's daddies. After months of secrecy, of course they would be curious.

Fitch was the shortest and smallest. He wore obscenely short shorts, a crop top, and a huge shit-eating grin. The other boy, who had to be Benji, was smiling at us. He had dark curly hair, dark haunted eyes.

Oh yes, definitely a Barbieri.

And Kylan stood in the middle of them, smiling shyly at us, his cheeks pink. "This is Benji, and you've met Fitch already."

"Hello," Benji said quietly.

Fitch, keeping his eyes on us, nudged Kylan. "Damn, Kysie. No wonder you beg for it."

Dominic sighed beside us. "Fitch, behave."

The look Fitch gave to Dominic was pure mischief

and daring. Definitely a brat. And from the way Dominic hummed, it was pretty obvious that was how he liked it.

Kylan turned to Fitch and tugged on Fitch's crop top. "You got the shirts, I see."

Fitch grinned and laughed, pulling on his crop top to show the big bold letters.

He had *small things* written across his front.

Then the three of them turned to Dominic and he rolled his eyes, and with a tired sigh, he turned around to show us the back. Sure enough, in much smaller print at his nape was *good things*.

Good things . . . small packages.

Oh god.

"I compromised," Dominic grumbled.

"You totally caved in," Nolan said with a smirk.

I got the feeling Dominic caved in a lot when it came to Fitch.

We joined them in the kitchen while the three boys sat on the sofa in a conjoined mess of limbs and giggles, Kylan in the middle of it all, talking low and all smiles. There weren't the words to explain how happy it made me.

Nolan held two empty wine glasses. "Can I get either of you a drink?" We both nodded, and Nolan poured two wines, then whispered, "He spoils Fitch rotten."

Dominic grumbled again. "Like you can talk."

"Like any of us can," Marek added.

It was true.

"So," Dominic said, nodding toward the three boys.

"A little birdie told me there are no more secrets, no more privacy clauses."

I smiled behind my wine glass. "A little birdie, huh? The little birdie next to our little birdie, I take it."

Dominic smirked. "He also said Ky's never been this happy."

Marek smiled up at me. "Same. It's been . . . a learning curve for all of us. We haven't decided when to announce anything publicly though, but no more secrets."

"It's . . ." I wasn't sure how to admit this. "It surprises me still just how much love a human heart can hold."

Me saying that clearly surprised them, though not Marek. He slid his arm around me and smiled at them. "Thank you for inviting us. It clearly means a lot to Kylan. He loves those boys."

We all looked over to the three boys, who paused their whispered chatter long enough to look at us.

Kylan's eyes met mine and the smile he gave me gave me butterflies.

It was so ridiculous.

"Thank you for coming," Nolan said quietly, seriously. "Benji really needed this. He needed them before the hearing this week."

Ah, yes . . .

The court case of the year.

"Kylan told you?" Nolan asked.

"A little," I replied. "He told us who Benji is, not much else. Never been gladder to be in property law, let me tell you."

Nolan's eyes drew over to the boys. He was watching Benji with such fondness, such turmoil.

"He'll be okay," Dominic murmured. "He'll get through this. You both will. As long as Benji has Fitch and Ky in his life, he'll be fine."

It was so true.

"Kylan needs them too," I said quietly.

Nolan conceded a nod. "Yeah, I know. I just . . . I'm worried for him. He has to face his father, and that won't be easy."

Jesus.

Dominic gave Nolan a clap on the arm. "No, it won't be. But you know what? Justice will prevail. It has to. That case is watertight, and that's all thanks to the bravery of Benji. He's got you, and he's got those two boys." Then he looked at the three boys with nothing but love. "We might have money and power, and we can pretend to be in charge of them, but those three boys are so much stronger than us. Pure grit and determination. They'll be fine."

They spoke a little of the court case after that, but conversation moved to other things. Dinner was great, the company, the mood.

But the best part for me was watching Kylan.

Watching him laugh, watching him chatter and be so animated.

Be so happy.

And at the end of the evening when Dominic suggested we do it all again soon, I readily agreed.

It didn't help that a sleepy Fitch was curled up on his

lap at the dining table, with his head in the crook of Dominic's neck. I wasn't sure if he was actually tired or just pretending to be so we'd all leave, but either way, it worked.

Nolan and Benji left at the same time, and the way the three boys hugged really tugged at my heart strings.

Kylan was quiet on the way home. I kept an eye on him in the rear-vision mirror. He was frowning out the window. "Everything okay, sweetheart?" I asked.

His eyes met mine in the mirror. "Yes, daddy. I'm fine."

Hmm.

He was in boy mode, and it didn't appear outwardly sexual. More that he needed reassurance and comfort.

"You're worried about Benji?"

His eyes flinched and he nodded. "Yes."

Marek turned in his seat so he could see him. "Did you want to sleep in our bed tonight?"

Kylan nodded quickly. "Yes, thank you, daddy." He smiled then. "In the middle of you is my favourite place."

Marek chuckled. "It's my favourite place for you to be too."

Kylan sighed, but then he squirmed, talking to Marek. "Actually, my very favourite place is when you hold me tight while daddy fucks me hard. That's my favouritest place."

Jesus.

"Can we do that when we get home?" Kylan asked, his eyes on mine in the rear-vision mirror. "Please, daddy? Pretty, pretty please?"

Fucking hell.

"Of course, baby doll," I said, voice low and rough. I was going to last all of twenty seconds at this rate. I shifted in my seat, trying to ease the ache, the draw down in my balls.

Marek chuckled beside me. "So, still want the nuclear family?"

Two boys?

I could barely handle one.

My mind went back to watching the three boys earlier tonight. Being bratty and giggly and as cute as they were, there was just no way.

"Absolutely not," I said. My gaze went to Kylan in the mirror. "There's only one boy for me."

"For us," Marek corrected, taking my hand and kissing my knuckles. "Only one boy for *us*."

Kylan grinned in the backseat. "I already said I won't share you. I need two daddies all to myself. I'm greedy and I'm not sorry."

I pulled into our car spot, put the car into Park, and cut the engine. "Good. Because tonight you're going to get us both."

He licked the corner of his mouth and very deliberately slid his hand to his crotch. "Thank you, daddy."

"Hm," I hummed, wondering if Fitch was beginning to wear off on him and also wondering why I wasn't mad about it. Kylan playing cute was hot. "Run along and get yourself ready. Wear whichever outfit you're feeling tonight."

He was out of the car in a flash and disappeared inside.

"Need a minute to calm down?" Marek asked me.

I laughed. "Or several. It's going to be over very fast tonight."

Marek laughed as we followed Kylan inside. Our home was so different to Dominic's. More artsy, more eclectic.

More us.

And I realised then that I didn't want to change a single thing. This was us, this was home.

I'd only had a sip of whisky before Kylan came down the stairs. He took careful, slow steps, barefoot but I could hear the buzz of a toy he clearly had embedded in his arse.

His outfit?

No pretty skirt, no pretty top.

The *only* thing he wore was a beaded a necklace, a smack of lip gloss, and a dangerous smirk.

He walked up to me and handed me the remote control for his vibrator. I loved the way he did this— handing over his control to me—it was more than symbolic. It was significant and something I'd never take for granted.

Marek came up behind him, his hands on Kylan's hips. "Look at this perfect baby doll, daddy," Marek whispered. Kylan closed his eyes, his cock thickening. "I think he needs his daddies to put him to bed."

I crushed my lips to Kylan's, tasting his strawberry lip

gloss, and when I pressed the higher setting on his remote control, he groaned into my mouth, his body trembling.

I broke the kiss, turned Kylan around, and with a handful of his hair, I tilted his head back. "Taste him, Marek. Taste his beautiful mouth."

Marek kissed him, delving his tongue in deep.

God, I could watch them kiss forever.

My dick, however, had other ideas. "Let's go tuck him in," I said. "And rock him to sleep."

"Oh," Kylan said, surprised. "We didn't watch my video yet."

Marek licked his lips. "Save it for tomorrow. You're tired."

Kylan hummed, a dreamy look in his eyes. "Carry me, daddy."

I scooped him up and carried him up the stairs, Marek hitting the lights behind us. The vibrator must have done a number on him because he clung to me, trembling, gasping, and whining.

"Shh," I said, laying him down on our bed. "Your daddies are here."

Kylan held his hand out for Marek. "Both of you."

Marek crawled onto the bed, pulling Kylan into his arms and holding him, spreading his legs wide for me. I unbuttoned my pants and pulled out my aching cock. "Always," I said, kneeling on the bed between Kylan's legs. "Both of us, always."

THIRTEEN
KYLAN

BENJI'S first court appearance was awful. I was so nervous and overwhelmed, I couldn't even imagine how Benji felt. So many suits, so many cops and lawyers, and people who stared.

So many reporters and cameras in his face, in his way. Intrusive, rude, and so disrespectful.

Loud and frightening.

I wore my new suit. A suit that Marek and Leon had taken me shopping for. It was from a ridiculously expensive upmarket store and they knew the tailor by name. I'd seen the price tag on a necktie and felt ill. Marek had tsked and ushered me to the suit section, telling Eduardo what I needed.

Marek knows suits, apparently. Leon watched on, nodding approvingly. And Eduardo was ever professional. He didn't even bat an eye when Marek introduced me as their boyfriend.

It was the first time in public with them and the first

time Marek had introduced me to anyone. It was a rush to hear him say it, and I'd been almost disappointed that Eduardo didn't seem fazed at all.

Almost.

But mostly relieved.

Marek had distracted me so I couldn't see how much Leon paid, and then we'd gone out for lunch.

As a throuple.

I kinda hated that word, but it was a good fit for us. It's what we were.

People didn't look twice at us. Whether they thought I was a nephew or their actual son, it didn't matter. It didn't matter what anyone else thought. Leon and Marek were proud to be with me, and with the confidence they exuded, it was hard not to feel that way too.

I felt so safe with them.

It also helped that Leon was no small man and he had a stare that could cut glass. With his aura of wealth and *do not fuck with me*, no one would have dared say anything.

Whether they knew it or not, they were creating a safety bubble for me that I felt totally secure in.

Which was probably what made the media at Benji's father's trial so scary to me.

Benji was ushered in with the DPP legal team and Nolan of course. I hated the way the media swarmed him. I was scared for him, panic clawing at my insides.

Standing there with Fitch outside the courthouse with all the mayhem, the chaos. The sheer fucking anxiety of it all. Fitch's eyes met mine, wide and as overwhelmed as me. He was normally so chill about everything, but even he was feeling it.

Then a large, warm hand pressed against my lower back and I turned, looking up and saw Leon. The hard set of his jaw, the serious edge to his gaze, watchful of the whole scene unfolding before us.

The relief I felt was immediate. My protector was here. No one could ever hurt me when he was with me.

I instinctively looked for Marek, finding him on the other side of Fitch. He had a different protective energy than Leon, gentler but no less intimidating.

The way he stood by Fitch, not touching but close enough to shield him from the chaos.

I can't believe I'd told them they didn't need to come with us . . .

Then Dominic appeared, his phone to his ear. He gave Marek a nod of thanks. "We need to go in," Dominic said to us. He slid his arm around Fitch's shoulders. Marek and Leon were on either side of me, and the five of us headed in.

Cameras clicked, reporters asked Dominic questions. They knew who he was, and I had no doubt, no doubt at all, that if they didn't know Leon and Marek—and Fitch and me—they would within the hour.

We sat a few rows behind Benji and Nolan.

He turned around, looking, searching, and visibly relaxed when he saw us. His father wasn't even going to be at this session, thank god.

I didn't want Benji to have to go through that. To

have that man sitting there, staring at him, knowing Benji was testifying against him.

I never wanted that piece of shit to be able to look at him ever again.

But the legal process, the formalities, the bullshit; I could barely follow any of it. I kept thinking about Leon's offer for me to study law, but I just couldn't see it.

This type of law?

Not for me.

When the session was over, I was surprised when everyone stood up. I was lost and dreading having to walk back outside into the throng of the bloodhound media.

"Are you okay?" Marek asked me quietly.

I nodded, though I'm sure he saw right through me.

"Okay, we need to go," Dominic said.

"What about Benji?" Fitch asked.

"He'll be fine. He'll meet us there." Dominic nodded to the end of the pew, signalling we should leave. I grabbed Fitch's hand, and with Marek on one side of us, Dominic at the other, and Leon at the front, we made our way back outside.

"Mr Ellington," one reporter said, shoving her microphone in Leon's face. "What are your ties to the Barbieri case? Who are these young men with you?"

"Mr Akhurst," another said, getting in Marek's way. "Can you explain . . ."

Yep.

They'd learned who they were.

Their faces, names would be on TV and in the papers. With me right beside them.

There was going public, and then there was *this* shitshow.

But Leon and Marek kept us walking, and Dominic gave some generic, cool-headed comment. We were shuffled into a waiting black van and the doors closing blocked out the noise.

The silence was deafening.

"Are you okay?" Leon said, taking my hand.

I nodded out of habit but then going with the truth, I shook my head. "I didn't like that. They knew who you were. They'll know who I am soon enough and wonder why you're with me." I looked back at the courthouse as the driver merged into traffic. "Where's Benji?"

"We're going back to Nolan's place," Leon said. "He'll meet us there."

"How do those reporters not get punched?" Fitch asked. Then he looked up at Dominic. "They pushed you!"

Dominic snorted. "I'm used to that."

God. I could never.

It seemed all I could do was shake my head. I didn't want to do this again.

"How often does Benji need to attend?" I asked. Leon, Marek, Dominic. Anyone. "Does he have to go all the time?"

Dominic answered. "No. The judge has agreed to video link."

"For his safety," Fitch added, frowning at me.

I stared at him. "What?"

"For the duration of the trial, he's supposed to be at

an undisclosed location," Dominic said. "It would be best if he doesn't have to see his father."

Or anyone in his father's mob connections...

I sighed, relieved. "Thank god for that. Where will he go? Is he leaving?" I turned to Leon and Marek. "I don't want him to leave."

"He'll be staying where he currently is," Dominic said. I realised that he didn't mention Nolan because the driver could hear us. "Though that may change if required."

Realisation sank in then that this was really fucking serious.

There were concerns for his life.

I sank into Leon's side and he tightened his hold on my hand.

Dominic let us into Nolan's place and as soon as we were inside, Marek pulled me in for a hug before he let go, only to put his hands to my face, scanning my eyes. "Are you okay?"

"I'm okay," I said. "Better now. I'll be a whole lot better when this is over."

Leon put his arms around the both of us, and I swear it was only then that I could breathe properly.

"Thank you both for being there today," I mumbled.

"Of course, sweetheart," Marek whispered.

"I couldn't do that kind of law," I admitted. "How do they defend the likes of Benji's father? How can they side with him? I'd get so fucking mad, I could just never . . ." They let me go just enough so I could look up at them both. "Maybe property law is more my style. More conveyancing and title deeds and less murder."

They both chuckled and Marek kissed my forehead, my cheek, my lips. "Anything you want, darling."

"Does that apply by proxy?" Fitch said from beside us. "Because if it does, anything *he* wants applies to anything *I* want. And I can make a list."

I snorted out a laugh and gave him a shove. "Shut up."

The front door opened then and Benji came in. Fitch and I collected him in a hug, barely letting Nolan in through the door. Benji was teary and sniffled, letting us hug him.

"Wanna go lie down?" Fitch asked, and Benji nodded.

He looked like he'd barely slept a wink the night before.

So Benji, Fitch, and I went into Nolan and Benji's bedroom, kicked out of our shoes and our jackets. "Never been so overdressed," Fitch said, throwing his jacket over the back of the chair in the corner. "Have you had sex on this chair?" he asked Benji. "I'll be very disappointed if you haven't."

Benji finally cracked half a smile. "Of course we have."

Fitch put his hand to his heart. "So proud."

He was such a brat and exactly what Benji needed right now.

The three of us climbed into bed, under the covers, with Benji in the middle. Until Fitch sat up, crawled over the both of us to snatch the remote control off the bedside closest to me. "You could have asked me to get it for you," I grumbled.

Benji laughed. "No he couldn't."

Fitch snuggled back down and, grinning, turned the TV on and began scrolling through channels. He found some mansion renovation show and settled in. "Oh, those tiles are terrible," Fitch said.

I ignored him and put my arm under Benji's head so I could cuddle him better, and that made Fitch reposition himself so he was using Benji's chest as a pillow.

"How you feeling, Benj?" I asked.

He sighed. "Glad today's over."

"I'm glad you don't have to be in the same room as him," I whispered.

"Me too."

"You were brave today," Fitch said. "Braver than I could have ever been."

"Same," I agreed.

"I wish I didn't have to be," Benji replied. "I'm grateful you're both here. And your partners."

Fitch popped his head up so he could look at me. "Marek was so hot today. Did you see how he totally swooped in to stand between me and the cameras?"

I smiled. "Yeah, I saw. Marek's hot every day."

"That little moustache is the sexiest fucking thing," Fitch said, putting his head back down and watching more of the TV show. "Oh, those tiles are worse. Who would allow that?"

Benji and I chuckled and then were quiet for a while,

watching the stupid show. He was right. Those tiles were worse.

"I'm so glad you two are here," Benji said eventually.

"Same," Fitch said, propping his head up again. "Because we need to talk to Kylan here, who was offered by those two hot-as-fuck daddies out there to be their live-in house boy and do nothing but float around the house all day in lingerie and stilettos—"

"It was a robe and slippers," I corrected.

Fitch wasn't deterred. "Close enough. And what did you tell them, Kylan? Tell Benji here what you told them."

I sighed.

"That's right," Fitch continued. "That he'd think about it. That he was considering university instead. Or an actual job." Fitch looked at me, confused. "Like honestly, what the fuck? You could be a totally kept boy, your own expense card, living in the lap of luxury in their gazillion dollar palace, doing nothing but having the best sex ever. And you want a nine-to-five?" He shook his head and let out a disappointed sigh. "Honestly, sign me the fuck up."

Benji chuckled again. "Maybe he wants to go to university. Leave him alone."

"I haven't decided," I told them. "They want me to move in with them, but I don't know."

They both looked at me, waiting.

"I don't want to rush things," I whispered. "But I also made a promise to you two, and I intend—"

"Ky," Benji murmured. "You have to do what's right for you. Look at me? I'm living here now."

"Because people were trying to kill you," I allowed. "That's different. And completely understandable. But I want to stay at the shithole apartment a couple nights a week with Fitch, make those solo videos, and try and make my own money. I need to try this. Sure, I could live with my daddies and want for nothing. Honestly, they have more money than the Reserve Bank. But I promised you both that we'd get through this together and that's what we're gonna do. I wouldn't have survived this long if it weren't for both of you."

Benji frowned. "Oh, Ky."

"I mean it," I said. "I know I haven't always acted like it, but you two saved my life. And I want to make good on the promise we made. Well, my part at least. I want to do all I can for the three of us, and this kinda feels like our one chance. Know what I mean?"

Benji nodded. "I get it. And I'm in, too. I don't know what I can do with the court case going on right now, but—"

"We got you covered," I told him. "We'll get you through this too, Benj. I promise."

Fitch brightened. "And if you have to go into witness protection, that means we all go. And we all get new identities, like the Three Musketeers: Buttercup, Blossom, and Bubbles."

Benji laughed. "That's the Powerpuff Girls."

"Close enough," I allowed.

Then Fitch frowned. "All this talk about leaving, not

leaving, going to university, or work," he said. "It's depressing."

"But we're not leaving," I said. "That's what I'm saying. We stick together no matter how things might change. We'll still be us."

Fitch made a face at me. "But uni? Or working a nine-to-five?" He sighed sadly. "I thought I raised you better than this."

I laughed and gave Fitch's shoulder a tweak. "Like I said, I still haven't decided. I thought maybe law school, but after today, definitely not criminal law. Maybe property law." I shrugged. "I could be their protégé. I would have the two best teachers in the country."

"Mmm, schoolboy and two teachers role play," Fitch said, happy again.

I chuckled. "It's more of a schoolgirl role play, but whatever."

Fitch shot me a look. "I've seen those photos. They're fucking hot."

Benji sighed. "You two are such whores."

"Thank you, baby," Fitch said easily, looking back at the TV. "Oh god, what is that wall colour? It has a warm undertone. It should be cool undertone to match the hideous tiles."

Benji and I laughed just as our four daddies appeared at the door.

"Hmm, I've seen porn like this," Fitch said. "Yes, please, and thank you."

Dominic sighed and the others smiled.

Leon and Marek were looking at me, warm and wonderful, making my insides flutter.

Benji sat up. "Nolan, can I hang out with these guys tomorrow?"

Nolan walked in. "Of course you can. You'll just need to be careful, that's all. Now that your name and face are everywhere, you probably shouldn't be hanging out on Oxford or Wylde Street."

"I don't want to go out anywhere," Benji said. "I just wanna hang out with these two."

"We can come here," I offered. "I know you're probably sick of staring at these walls but Nolan's right. It's safer and it's not forever. We'll do something fun."

Fitch got excited. "We can bring the camera set up and film some solos."

Benji shoved him. "You're not doing anything on our bed. Jesus Christ."

Fitch nodded to the chair. "I'll use the sex chair."

"It's not—" Benji said.

"Oh god—" Nolan said at the same time.

Dominic and Leon both laughed.

I got out of the bed and collected my shoes and my jacket. "Fitch, get out. Benji needs a nap, and you need . . ." I turned to Dominic. "He needs some discipline. I would say punishment, but we all know he'd enjoy that more."

Fitch shoved his jacket and shoes into Dominic's arms. "I'm not even going to try and deny that. Thanks, Kysie."

Dominic smirked, his gaze full of nothing but love. "Home time?"

Fitch beamed up at him. "Yes, please."

Marek took my jacket and shoes, and Leon put his arm around me. "We'll see ourselves out," he said to Nolan.

Nolan gave a nod. "Thanks again for today."

"No problem at all. If you need anything, you have my number."

"See you tomorrow, Benj," I said. "Text me if you want me to bring anything."

He looked about ready to fall asleep but he smiled, and Leon led me out the door. "Let's get you home, princess."

I smiled and leaned into him, and as we climbed into a taxi, I couldn't help but think of that one word.

Home.

What it used to mean, and what it meant now. The place that felt right, the people who made it so.

"So I was thinking," I said as we walked into the grand hall to the living room. The opulent furniture, the grandiosity of it all used to seem so over the top; now it felt like home.

"Thinking about what?" Marek asked as he laid my suit jacket neatly on the back of the sofa.

"About my future. About us. About the word home."

They both stopped and waited.

"I was thinking I could stay here four nights a week and stay with Fitch the other three. Our lease is up in about four months, so that kinda feels like a great trial period for us to see if living together forever, and for real, would be good. And who knows, maybe after that, we can sign our lease for another six months but keep it as a studio for our Only Fans, and maybe as a bit of a boy's club if me, Fitch, and Benji want to hang out and watch movies some nights. I don't know. I haven't run this past them, so I'm not sure. Hopefully our videos will start earning some money and we can afford that."

I waited for them to object to being able to *afford* anything, but they didn't.

They just smiled.

So I kept talking. "And maybe I can take some courses in the second half of the year to get me ready for university next year. I'm not ready for it this year, but with some practice and bridging courses, I could really hit the ground running next year. I think I'd be better suited to property law and you two are like the gurus of that, and I should have some income by then, so I'll feel better about contributing . . ."

They were still smiling.

"What?" I asked. "You're not saying anything. Did I say something wrong?"

Leon broke first, his grin wide. "Of course you didn't. You just said *forever*. You said *living together forever*." He looked at Marek. "Did you hear that?"

He nodded, smiling. "I believe so, yes. He definitely said *living together forever, for real*. That's what I heard."

I chuckled. "Did you not hear anything else I said after that?"

Leon nodded and cupped my jaw. "We heard it all,

darling. You can be whatever you want, do whatever you want, whenever you're ready. You can make decisions, you can change your mind, you can change direction, you can do whatever makes you happy. No rush, no pressure."

Leon came up to stand behind me. He pressed his lips to my neck. "But you did say *forever*."

"And I meant it," I said. "Fitch and Benji are my brothers, my family. But you're my daddies, my home. I don't know what my future looks like. The fact I am even thinking of my future is a miracle and a testament to you both and how you love me. There's still a lot I don't know, and things could change. But we won't. What we have is forever. I have to believe that." I swallowed hard. "As long as I have you both, I'll be home."

Leon kissed me softly. "My sweetest boy. You said the word forever again."

Marek hummed, his hands on my hips. He looked up at Leon. "Should I get him our gift? We were going to wait, but I think we should give it to him now."

Leon nodded. "Yes, we should."

Marek disappeared and I looked up at Leon. "A gift? What for? It's not my birthday."

He booped his finger on the tip of my nose. "We wanted to give you something to show you what you mean to us."

Marek came back with a small box. "We considered getting you a necklace and threading our wedding bands on it so you could carry our commitment around with you," he said. "But we agreed that it didn't feel right to not wear our wedding bands. So we got you this."

He handed me the box. It was a jewellery box but bigger than a ring box.

My heart was squeezing out each beat, my hands were shaking. I opened it, and inside were two plain thin gold bands and a third with a large pink stone. I looked up at them both. "What is . . . ? I don't understand . . ."

"One for each of us," Leon said. He took the biggest plain ring and slid it onto his ring finger next to his wedding band, and then Marek took the other plain ring and did the same.

Which left the pink one for me. "Is this mine?" I whispered. "It's so pretty."

"Pretty for our pretty one," Marek said.

Leon took the ring and took my left hand, sliding it onto my ring finger. "We can't make this legal, but we sure as hell can make the same promise to you."

I was so stunned, so shocked. So emotional. I couldn't take my eyes off it. "Is it pink topaz? It's just so pretty! I love it. I love you both. This is perfect."

Marek chuckled. "No, darling. It's not a topaz. It's a pink diamond."

I stared at him, then at Leon, at the ring, and back to them. I could feel the colour draining from my face, and I could not form the words to tell them . . .

This must have cost so much money. Too much money. Far too much . . .

Leon laughed and took my hand, kissing my new ring. "You won't lose it, you *can* accept it, you *can* wear it, you *do* deserve it. Did I cover everything you were about to say?"

The only response I was capable of was to burst into tears and nod.

They held me tight, both kissing the sides of my head. "Is this kind of forever okay, princess?" Marek murmured.

I nodded, crying some more. "'S perfect." I looked up at them, tears and all, hiding nothing. "Please take me upstairs. I need to be naked and in between you both for hours and hours."

Leon laughed and hoisted me up onto his hips. "Whatever our princess wants," he said, walking up the stairs as if I weighed nothing.

Marek followed us up, grinning at me. "Our princess gets."

EPILOGUE - KYLAN
SIX MONTHS LATER

"WE DID IT!" Fitch cried, holding his laptop. "Look! Come take a look! We fucking did it."

Benji and I both went to him, leaned in, and looked at the screen.

One hundred thousand followers.

When we'd taken our Only Fans public, we'd set goals. Realistic goals, normal goals, and stupid crazy goals. We'd laughed and wrote down dream income, dream follower numbers, dream rankings, all written down on a whiteboard in our small and dingy apartment.

We'd blown all the realistic goals out of the water in the first month.

It was absurd how fast it happened.

We'd exceeded every goal we'd set for ourselves. And the outlandish goals we'd written down as an impossible joke? We smashed those too.

It was more money than I could have ever dreamed possible. And we hadn't just renewed our lease. We'd bought the damn apartment. Well, the three of us had paid a decent deposit and were paying it off.

It helped to have *the* Leon Ellington and Marek Akhurst do the contract negotiations and working out our legal property contract between me, Fitch and Benji. We set up a company, The Wylde Street Boys, sorted everything out properly and legally. Four lawyer daddies made a very strong team, and our little apartment had become our studio and our head office. We had it painted, a still tiny but brand-new kitchen installed, new bathroom fixtures.

And it was ours.

Well, the mortgage was ours, but we had a smart repayment plan, and we were making amazing money to even have it paid off early. It all seemed so surreal.

We'd really focused on our business after Benji's first day in court. The media had gone crazy, and he'd needed the distraction and something else to focus his energy on.

He'd suggested a marketing strategy, working out plans and spreadsheets on percentages, income, and expenditure allocations. Fitch worked on social media accounts for our page, and I concentrated on editing and producing our content.

We made a damn good team.

I still had plans for studying. That hadn't changed. I was taking some introduction courses to help prepare me for university in the new year.

I was excited to start. I would be almost a good eight years older than most of my classmates, but I didn't care. None of them had walked in my shoes. None of them had been homeless and found themselves renting out their bodies to afford food.

And none of them had two daddies who were at the top of the field we'd be studying. Two daddies who helped me, tutored me, encouraged me.

Two daddies who believed in me.

They were so fucking proud of me. They'd never questioned my desire to do the Only Fans content. Once I'd told them about my need for my own success and my own financial stability, they'd given nothing but full support.

They also loved my videos.

They'd even watched me film a few of them.

The video of me finishing on a vibrating dildo before an *anon daddy* appeared on-screen to undo his jeans, grab my hips, and pump a quick load deep into my arse was my most popular and rewatched content.

Leon was still smug about that.

Fitch still talked about it.

And Benji . . . Benji was doing okay. His father's trial had been hard on him, but he was proud of himself for seeing it through. We were all so fucking proud of him.

Bruno Barbieri had been sentenced to three concurrent life sentences for murder, conspiracy to murder, amongst other charges as well.

He would never see the outside world again. He'd also had to be confined to solitary because two other inmates had already tried to kill him.

Nothing he didn't deserve, in my eyes.

But Benji's brother's case for fraud and tax evasion

was about to begin. It was an open and closed case according to Dominic and Nolan, but still . . . I wouldn't stop worrying until that piece of shit was behind bars too.

And probably not even then.

They weren't just my friends and business partners. They were my brothers.

So I knew when something was up with one of them. "Benj, what's the matter?" I asked. "You're distracted and you keep checking your watch. Do you need to be somewhere? We can finish up here if you need to go."

His eyes met mine and he let out a nervous laugh. "I, uh . . . I asked Nolan to call Leon and Marek, and Dominic was—"

Someone knocked on the door, and Benji laughed nervously before running to open it. Sure enough Leon, Marek, Dominic, and Nolan walked in.

Fitch stood up. "What's going on? Is this a surprise orgy, because as hot as that would be, no one fucks me but Dominic." He shrugged. "I will totally watch you guys though."

Benji laughed and slid his hand into Nolan's. "No, this is not an orgy, Fitch. You fucking perv."

Dominic went to him and gave him a rough hug and kiss on the forehead. "Behave, brat."

"Do you know what's going on?" Fitch asked everyone.

I sure as hell didn't, and Leon and Marek both shook their heads as they came to stand next to me. "No, Dominic didn't say what it was."

Fitch gasped and pulled away from Dominic. "*You* know what this is?"

Dominic put his finger to his lips. "Shh."

We turned to Benji and Nolan, who were smiling, nervous. "So," Benji said. "I'd planned to change my name, back when we'd first discussed ditching my surname, and I'd joked about changing my name from Benito Barbieri to Benji O'Brien." He let out a laugh. "Taking Nolan's surname."

"So, we thought we'd do it officially," Nolan added. "Today. At the private function room at Club 180. Which is basically next door, so if you'd like to join us. There's a celebrant waiting." He checked his watch. "Uh, now."

I was stunned.

I turned to Fitch . . . who was mad? "Marriage licenses take thirty days, Benji," he said. "Are you telling me you've been planning this for thirty days and didn't tell me? Not once? Not even a little hint?"

Benji made an awkward smile. "Uh, surprise?"

Fitch growled, then turned on Dominic. "And you knew!"

He raised both hands. "I knew half an hour ago when Nolan asked me to get Leon and Marek."

Fitch pouted at Dominic and then at Benji.

"Would it make you feel better if you were my best man?" Benji asked. He looked at me then. "Both of you. Please?"

I nodded. "Of course."

"But I'm the bestest best man," Fitch declared. Then

he levelled a glare at Dominic. "And I'd just like to point out, for no particular reason at all, no siree, no *reason* at all, that I will be the only one without a ring on my finger." He raised one eyebrow. "And cock rings don't count, just so you know." He held up his left hand. "Ring. Finger."

Dominic sighed.

Leon and Marek both chuckled, and Nolan covered his laugh with a cough. But Benji and I laughed. "Come on, brat," I said, turning Fitch toward the door and, with my arm around his shoulder, led him out.

We were ushered inside 180 to the private function room where a man in a blue suit with bright orange glasses and a huge smile was waiting. Benji and Nolan had a brief and lovely ceremony. No fanfare, no pizzazz, just a whole lot of love.

There was champagne for the grown-ups and mock-tails for us boys, fancy food, and light jazz music.

And one very happy, very in-love Benji O'Brien.

I thumbed the ring on my finger absentmindedly. "You look so happy," I said to Benj. "I'm so happy for you, Benj. You deserve this."

He nodded, a little teary. "Don't regret your no-contract rule?" he asked, nodding to the table where he'd signed his marriage certificate.

I couldn't marry Leon and Marek. We all knew that. But I wore their ring on my finger, a symbol of their unconditional love. It was all I needed. "Nah, I'm good without it."

Benji's smile became a grin. "You really are." Then he sighed. "We did okay, didn't we? Us three?"

"Oh, baby, we did better than okay. Look at us." I gestured to Fitch, who was talking to Marek and Dominic, making Marek laugh. But Dominic was looking at him with hearts in his eyes. "How long do you think until Fitch has that man's ring on his finger?"

"By tonight," Benji answered. "He'll pout and sulk, and that'll be that."

I chuckled and sipped my drink. "I'm proud of us," I said quietly.

Benji's eyes met mine. "Me too."

Fitch appeared beside us. "What are we talking about?"

"Us," I replied. "The three musketeers . . . three blind mice . . . three—"

"Three little come bunnies," Fitch added.

Benji laughed. "Don't ever change, Fitch."

I held my mocktail up and we clinked our glasses. "To the Wylde Street Boys."

"To us," Benji said.

"To mostly me," Fitch said. Then he sighed dramatically. "Fine. To us, because we're awesome. Whatever."

THE END

ABOUT THE AUTHOR

N.R. Walker is an Australian author who loves her genre of queer romance. First published in 2012, she now has over 70 books, many which are also audiobooks, and numerous translations done in nine different languages.

She loves writing and spends far too much time doing it but wouldn't have it any other way.

---

nrwalker.net

ALSO BY N.R. WALKER

Merry Christmas Cupid

To the Moon and Back

Second Chance at First Love

Outrun the Rain

Into the Tempest

Touch the Lightning

EWB - Enemies With Benefits

Holiday Heart Strings

Bloom

The Men from Echo Creek

Method Acting

The Bait

Nothing Left to Lose

Deck the Fire Halls

Benji

Fitch

TITLES IN AUDIO:

Cronin's Key

Cronin's Key II

Cronin's Key III

Red Dirt Heart

Red Dirt Heart 2

Sir

Tallowwood

Imago

Throwing Hearts

Sixty Five Hours

Taxes and TARDIS

The Dichotomy of Angels

The Hate You Drink

Pieces of You

Pieces of Me

Pieces of Us

Tic-Tac-Mistletoe

Lacuna

Bossy

Code Red

Learning to Feel

Dearest Milton James

Dearest Malachi Keogh

Three's Company

Christmas Wish List

Code Blue

Davo

The Kite

Learning Curve

Merry Christmas Cupid

To the Moon and Back

Second Chance at First Love

Outrun the Rain

Into the Tempest

Touch the Lightning

EWB

Holiday Heart Strings

Bloom

The Men from Echo Creek

Method Acting

The Bait

Deck the Fire Halls

Benji

Fitch

SERIES COLLECTIONS:

Red Dirt Heart Series

Turning Point Series

Thomas Elkin Series

Spencer Cohen Series

Imago Series

Blind Faith Series

Missing Pieces Series

The Storm Boys Series

Gay Sex Club Stories

FREE READS:

Sixty Five Hours

Learning to Feel

His Grandfather's Watch (And The Story of Billy and Hale)

The Twelfth of Never (Blind Faith 3.5)

Twelve Days of Christmas (Sixty Five Hours Christmas)

Best of Both Worlds

TRANSLATED TITLES:

ITALIAN

Fiducia Cieca (Blind Faith)

Attraverso Questi Occhi (Through These Eyes)

Preso alla Sprovvista (Blindside)

Il giorno del Mai (Blind Faith 3.5)

Cuore di Terra Rossa Serie (Red Dirt Heart Series)

Natale di terra rossa (Red dirt Christmas)

Intervento di Retrofit (Elements of Retrofit)

A Chiare Linee (Clarity of Lines)

Senso D'appartenenza (Sense of Place)

Spencer Cohen Serie (including Yanni's Story)

Punto di non Ritorno (Point of No Return)

Punto di Rottura (Breaking Point)

Punto di Partenza (Starting Point)

Imago (Imago)

Imagines

Il desiderio di un soldato (A Soldier's Wish)

Scambiato (Switched)

Tallowwood

The Hate You Drink

Ho trovato te (Finders Keepers)

Cuori d'argilla (Throwing Hearts)

Galassie e Oceani (Galaxies and Oceans)

Il peso di tut (The Weight of it All)

Pieces of You - Missing Pieces 1

Pieces of Me - Missing Pieces 2

Pieces of Us - Missing Pieces 3

Code Red

FRENCH

Confiance Aveugle (Blind Faith)

A travers ces yeux: Confiance Aveugle 2 (Through These Eyes)

Aveugle: Confiance Aveugle 3 (Blindside)

À Jamais (Blind Faith 3.5)

Cronin's Key Series

Au Coeur de Sutton Station (Red Dirt Heart)

Partir ou rester (Red Dirt Heart 2)

Faire Face (Red Dirt Heart 3)

Trouver sa Place (Red Dirt Heart 4)

Le Poids de Sentiments (The Weight of It All)

Un Noël à la sauce Henry (A Very Henry Christmas)

Une vie à Refaire (Switched)

Evolution (Evolved)

Galaxies & Océans

Qui Trouve, Garde (Finders Keepers)

Sens Dessus Dessous (Upside Down)

La Haine au Fond du Verre (The hate You Drink)

Tallowwood

Spencer Cohen Series

Thomas Elkin One

Lacuna

GERMAN

Flammende Erde (Red Dirt Heart)

Lodernde Erde (Red Dirt Heart 2)

Sengende Erde (Red Dirt Heart 3)

Ungezähmte Erde (Red Dirt Heart 4)

Vier Pfoten und ein bisschen Zufall (Finders Keepers)

Ein Kleines bisschen Versuchung (The Weight of It All)

Ein Kleines Bisschen Fur Immer (A Very Henry Christmas)

Weil Leibe uns immer Bliebt (Switched)

Drei Herzen eine Leibe (Three's Company)

Über uns die Sterne, zwischen uns die Liebe (Galaxies and Oceans)

Unnahbares Herz (Blind Faith 1)

Sehendes Herz (Blind Faith 2)

Hoffnungsvolles Herz (Blind Faith 3)

Verträumtes Herz (Blind Faith 3.5)

Thomas Elkin: Verlangen in neuem Design

Thomas Elkin: Leidenschaft in klaren

Thomas Elkin: Vertrauen in bester Lage

Traummann töpfern leicht gemacht (Throwing Hearts)

Sir

So Unendlich Viel Liebe (To the Moon and Back)

THAI

Sixty Five Hours (Thai translation)

Finders Keepers (Thai translation)

SPANISH

Sesenta y Cinco Horas (Sixty Five Hours)

CHINESE

Blind Faith

Bossy

JAPANESE

Bossy

To the Moon and Back

PORTUGUESE

Sessenta e Cinco Horas